The Furrow

Published by special arrangment with Éditions Le Tripode, France in conjunction with their duly appointed agents Books and More Agency.

Library and Archives Canada Cataloguing in Publication

Title: The furrow / Valérie Manteau ; translated from the French by Claire Foster.
Other titles: Sillon. English
Names: Manteau, Valérie, 1985- author. | Foster, Claire (Translator), translator
Description: Translation of: Le sillon. | Includes bibliographical references.
In English, translated from the French.
Identifiers: Canadiana (print) 20260225851 | Canadiana (ebook) 2026022815X
ISBN 9781778430893 (softcover) | ISBN 9781778430909 (EPUB)
Subjects: LCGFT: Novels.
Classification: LCC PQ2713.A58 S5513 2026 | DDC 843/.92—dc23

Edited by Eugenie Dalland
Cover design by CHIPS
Cover image: "The Weary Messenger," Louis Fleckenstein, 1910.
J Paul Getty Museum
Interior design by Megan Fildes

Invisible Books is committed to protecting our natural environment. As part of our efforts, both the cover and interior of this book are printed on acid-free 100% post-consumer recycled fibres.

Printed and bound in Canada.

Invisible Books | Halifax, Picton, Saint John

www.invisiblebooks.ca

Published with the generous assistance of the Canada Council for the Arts, the Ontario Arts Council, and the Government of Canada.

Cet ouvrage a bénéficié du soutien du Programme d'aide à la publication de l'Institut français.

Canada Council for the Arts Conseil des Arts du Canada
ONTARIO ARTS COUNCIL
CONSEIL DES ARTS DE L'ONTARIO
an Ontario government agency
un organisme du gouvernement de l'Ontario
Canada

The Furrow

Valérie Manteau

translated from the French by Claire Foster

INVISIBLE BOOKS
Halifax | Picton | Saint John

Do you know what it means to sentence someone to live a dove's life of constant worry?

—HRANT DINK (1954–2007)

On the little square in front of the restaurants there's a building, it looks like a church. That's where I am, waiting for you outside. It's ridiculous, I walk past this place all the time and before today had never noticed the steeple. Journalist Ece Temelkuran writes that selective blindness is the malady of contemporary Turkey, so here I am, I guess, distracted as a Turk. According to Temelkuran, if you ask passersby who built all these churches right in the heart of Anatolia's cities, they dodge the question, too overwhelmed by the unnerving strangeness of the churches' silhouettes—*they're practically prehistoric!* Saint Euphemia: the name is nearly illegible, but definitely not prehistoric. Waiting for Sara, I enter the church to investigate, but inside, everything's in Greek. I consult the internet. Wikipedia won't open, blocked for months now by the government. Other sites serve as workarounds. Founded in 685 B.C. by the Greeks on the south side of the Bosphorus, Chalcedon saw the birth of its younger sister and rival, Byzantium, on the other side of the strait. Both cities prospered. Chalcedon was, in dizzying succession, Megarian, Persian, Macedonian, Bithynian, Romanian, then back to Persian, then back again to Romanian, then Arab, before falling into the hands of the Ottomans more than a century before the fall of Constantinople. Chalcedon kept its Greek name and mixed population—Latin, Armenian, Jewish—until the beginning of the twentieth century. After the dissolution of the

Ottoman Empire, the Greeks who were expelled under the Treaty of Lausanne founded, in Greece, two Nea Chalkidona orphans: the Chalcedon of the Bosphorus became Kadıköy, "the Judge's Village," which in 1930 was incorporated into the new municipality of Istanbul. This is how an Armenian Gregorian church now stands alongside a Greek Orthodox church named after a local martyr from the third century, Euphemia. Whether she was beheaded or condemned to wild beasts remains unclear. Legend has it that once a year, on September 16, blood flows from her tomb. The Persians tried to burn relics to put an end to this phenomenon, but this attempt earned them only more blood, and the saint, intact, is said to have performed a second miracle some centuries later.

When we met, Sara was living in the leftist bastion where I now live. She was renting a large apartment in which roommates of short- and medium-term would come and go, a mix of locals and foreigners, a common practice in the city since Istanbul rent and national wage averages have for a long time had nothing to do with each other. But despite everything, Turkey was—with panache and a few hiccups—pulling itself out of the economic dip of the early 2000s. Secular Istanbul was split between two sides and had begun to abandon the European side of the Bosphorus, mired as it was in nostalgia, to embrace the Asian side, where cafés, galleries, and tattoo parlours were flourishing. On summer evenings, beers in hand, we'd sit on the rocks of the waterfront at sunset and, with narrowed eyes, look out at the old Byzantium, Hagia Sophia, and the Blue Mosque, all abandoned to tourists. We should have remembered that, here, sometimes the surf causes damage. It wasn't for nothing that Zeus thought it useful to make an example of

Prometheus by chaining him to the Caucasus Mountains, probably not unlike the ones on which Noah, in his ark, had taken refuge, contemplating the sinful humanity of Anatolia swept away by the waves.

Arab Spring in the south, Indignados in the north, Turkey of the 2010s was reeling on Taksim Square. It was the setting for a spectacular outbreak of revolt against the conservative government that will be remembered for one name: the previously insignificant Gezi Park, engraved in marble on the Armenian cemetery that preceded it, went down in history for having been sold to developers by Recep Tayyip Erdoğan, former mayor of Istanbul turned prime minister, who was then preparing to be elected president of the Republic. International commentators, as well as most of the local ones, who had complacently encouraged Erdoğan when he claimed to be on the path to democracy, remained hesitant to change their tune in the face of the brutal repression that was demonstrated at Gezi Park. It was a short night for Le Grand Soir—a teenager hit by a tear gas grenade that had been thrown by the police celebrated his fifteenth birthday in a coma before eventually succumbing to his injuries. Erdoğan, drunk with vengeance and determined to crush the rebels, had his supporters boo the victim's family. The peaceful sit-in organized in protest was violently attacked by the police. In 2013, hopes of bringing democracy into the country were stifled by tear gas, and since 2015, it's been war all over again. With the breakdown of the peace process in Kurdistan, Syria is in turmoil, and the most conservative policies have been reinstated at the highest levels of government like it's 1940. Sara, newly graduated from a program for post-traumatic stress disorder therapy, left Istanbul to settle on the Syrian border alongside refugees from a conflict that we were at the time only just beginning to understand would persist and spread further out—that was barely two years ago now. Two years, I'm telling you, and this is the psychologist talking now, it's too much. I'm going crazy in Gaziantep. It's simple, by the way, I spend my time sending home aid workers who lose it after six months, a year, I'm extremely good at detecting the first signs of burnout in other people and guess what, the first signs and also all the subsequent ones, I've got 'em all. I cry all the time even when we have sex I can't help it—sorry habibi but it's true, I can say it, can't I. Next to Sara, Ibrahim jumps but doesn't say a word, he listens, his eyes elsewhere, a vague, polite smile, and I begin to wonder if he understands English, whether he's been following our conversation at all. I don't know why she insisted on introducing him to me, and I wonder if it's because of him that we're drinking tea in a bar that doesn't serve alcohol. I hope they don't have anything to announce. I turn toward him when I ask questions about their life in Gaziantep, and he seems to want to temper things a little, but Sara cuts him off and adds yet more intensity by speaking much more loudly than necessary, the Turks, the Kurds, the Syrians, the pseudo-humanitarian workers, all of them can go to hell in their fertile crescent of shit—this land is cursed, we should run for our lives. Of course, I wonder where we could even go. Not to France anyway, no thank you, things don't seem to be going very well in your country either. European hypocrisy makes me sick. The U.S., I'd sooner hang myself. I really ought to find myself a Canadian, but I can't help it—here she looks a little sorry, and Ibrahim notices—I like the men from here. At this, Ibrahim smiles. I think to myself that I hope for his sake that Ibrahim likes roller coasters because, she's quick to add, taking out a cigarette, it's a mystery to me, in any case.

She goes out to smoke and now I'm alone with Ibrahim. I don't know what he knows about her, or me, if he knows that she and I used to be together, he asks me now if I'm seeing anyone in Istanbul. When I landed at Sara's apartment back in 2013 I was broke, whenever I travelled I'd stay on friends' or friends of friends' couches and, if I didn't know anyone, would use social networking sites for travellers on a budget. It was on one of those sites that I met Sara. It was essentially a classified ad: queer psychologist, involved in social movements, supported the democratization of the country, that's all I knew, and it was more than enough to give me the best possible introduction to Istanbul, about which I knew nothing. I basically thought the Asian side would be a sort of Chinatown. She laughed, incredulous, no one taught you in school that this side of the Bosphorus is Asia? Except yes, we'd studied all the geopolitical subtleties that were supposed to prove that Turkey had no place in the European Union. On the way to her apartment from the airport, I had to take a bus, get off under a bridge on a highway, then walk through a succession of residential neighbourhoods, take the third right, then the fourth left, then past the grocery store go down the stairs and turn right and there it was, ring the bell, number 34. I'd carefully written all this into a notebook only to forget the notebook in Marseille, remembering just that the name of the bridge in question was something *köprüsü*, except that *köprüsü*, in Turkish, means bridge. The driver of the bus and a kind passenger who acted as my interpreter, both in hysterics, called Sara so she could explain where it was I was going, and the entire bus had basically transformed into an honour guard by the time we finally arrived at the right bridge. I'd gained the company of an old man who insisted on carrying my suitcase down the steps and who left only when he was sure I wasn't lost anymore, and I didn't know how to say anything in Turkish, not even thank you, and I was afraid he'd become overbearing, but soon I realized he didn't want a thing—only that my trip get off to a good start. Then, alone on that little street, holding my suitcase at the bottom of stairs freshly painted with the colours of the rainbow, the colours of Gezi, I wondered what the hell I was doing there. Now, three years later, I live just a few streets away and know these steps by heart, and they have, after months of back-and-forth between the artist–activists and the police, returned to grey, and I can no longer summon my first feeling of Istanbul. But that first night at Sara's remains, in my memory, as pink and sparkling as the first notes of a romance. I hadn't come to Istanbul to start a revolution nor to drink myself silly on a couch, I had plans to visit the Hagia Sophia first thing the next morning—but as soon as I arrived I discovered the slow tempo of long evenings spent drinking rakı, remaking the world with my hosts. Sara folded me into her, and at dawn I woke up covered in red curls.

About Taksim, the epicentre of the protests, novelist Aslı Erdoğan writes: "Taksim Square belongs to us, those who died there, to everyone ... and every time we march toward this unrecognizable square, despite the batons, water cannons, and tear gas, every time we take that path, it will be *ours*." Now it's always under construction (no one knows why and no one really cares), and I feel like it belongs more to the pigeons than to collective memory. Once there were tents everywhere, on both sides of an alleyway called Hrant Dink Street, named after an Armenian journalist who'd been killed a few years earlier and had now been adopted as a symbolic figure by the protesters who were occupying the square to prevent its destruction, since it was one of the few green spaces left in the city. In the middle of the police line were musicians, artists, young and old people of all kinds, hippies, hipsters, white-collar workers, Islamists. A blues band with a confident, androgynous singer with a side shave and a bearded accordionist, both of them totally owning the scene—it was unforgettable. A young woman, standing a little apart from the crowd, organized the performances, standing on a stepladder like a sculpture, a Turkish flag in each hand, arms outstretched, and she seemed, beneath her helmet of black hair, to be marshalling the assembly between two police raids. One day, after being teargassed in the face, she fainted and was never seen again at the encampment. Outbursts of violence and solidarity followed. When the police charged, there was a stampede in the pedestrian street, the crowd rushed to take shelter and all the shops opened their doors to let people in—all except Mado, the ice cream chain, which barricaded itself behind its iron bars, securing the lasting hatred of the Gezi generation. There was one guy in particular who I spotted several times—tall, tattooed, delicate, helpful, friendly, very friendly to women in general and to me just a little extra. Enough for me to walk down the street trying to look casual where he and a few friends had set up a squat in a clothing store that had been commandeered by the protesters. Sara remembers the place well—it's a newspaper now, isn't it?—but not the guy. It feels to her like a lifetime ago. Everyone wants to leave, you know, Istanbul is hell, I don't even recognize the neighbourhood anymore, and have you seen how high rent has gotten? We're sort of stuck here,

Ibrahim, his Syrian passport, he can't get very far—but at least he's got a passport. And you! What were you thinking, coming here? I shrug. I'd quit my job and thought the chaos of Istanbul would keep my mind occupied. And then there's that guy— Sara cuts me off, bangs her fist on the table, startling Ibrahim: you're fucking a Turk?

So, what's new in the country of human rights? I wonder if he's being sarcastic, but no. I try to keep up with the French press, but it seems outrageously useless and self-centred if you don't live in the middle of Paris—if you are, for example, on a balcony in the middle of Istanbul. What are today's big headlines? Two ministers resigned last week—economy and culture. Major political crisis, split within the left, big drama. And now we learn they're together and have chosen, as their first political act following their revolution, to take a romantic selfie in San Francisco.

No kidding? I show him a photograph of the two ministers taking selfies on a hill overlooking the water. He squints, visibly disappointed, oh, I thought it'd be two men, that would've been at least a little bit interesting. Then he quotes Nietzsche, this little pedant: "Is the press anything more than an everlasting false alarm?"

Seriously, what does France even represent in the world nowadays. Human rights? We're rotting in decadence, lobotomized by television and fear, kitsch everywhere all the time, culturally and politically dead as a doornail, yet still there are people turning their ears to us as if we're some big beautiful humanist voice?

He rolls his cigarettes with care, bites his lips out of impatience to smoke while trying to listen to me, tapping his foot to the rhythm of a song that must be playing in his head, behind all my bullshit. It's early and I'm still in pyjamas, coffee on the table, taking my time before really starting the day—for which I barely have anything planned in the first place. After reading some of the paper I'll do my daily Assimil *Turkish* lesson, I study without progressing through dialogues in which one learns how to apologize for not having prepared dinner for one's husband and how to not get angry in a traffic jam; since I neither cook nor drive, I don't retain a thing. I'd like to be able to read at least Twitter, which, in the absence of free press, is the only properly updated news source in this country. He's already tied his sneakers and put rings on his fingers when he tucks the first rolled cigarette behind his ear. He'll smoke it downstairs with the tea vendor before taking his motorcycle out of the room that serves as a garage, it's an expensive BMW he bought on a whim, an impulse born of childish frustration that his revolution didn't work out. He rolls another cigarette for later, after which he'll go to the Muz, a former squat turned café that also houses a satirical newspaper.

What makes France such an important symbol that the whole world rose up for *Charlie*? I pronounce *Charlie* with the French accent, the soft *ch* and the open *a*, *Charlie* which most Turks simply call *Hebdo*. He grimaces. That had nothing to do with France. I'm not so sure. But then again, what kind of response would have been the right one? He pauses, checks that he has his keys and lighter in his pockets, gets up. What can we do for freedom, art, love? It's a simple question, isn't it?

Sara went back to Gaziantep with Ibrahim, we barely had a moment alone together. She declares that we must schedule regular calls with each other, starting now. She's worried about me because I was stupid enough to tell her that since I'd arrived in Turkey, I'd swapped out my regular psychoanalysis for yoga classes and wasn't finding myself that much worse off—apart from, of course, recurring nightmares and bouts of crippling anxiety. Voices, too. Now, *never* say, even to a friend, especially not to a psychologist friend, that you're hearing voices. I mean I hear voices in my head, Sara, it's nothing, just like a little speech bubble with music notes inside. Because I'm alone every day. And I want to hear *someone* speak to me in my mother tongue. It's in French, then, you know who it is? It depends: people who exist, or don't, the dead, the living, too, the occasional poem or passage. And you think you can tell the difference between these voices and real life? Yeah, yeah. I can't have her start policing me now. Have you signed the petition for the girl in Adana? I'll send it to you. Immediately I see the email appear in my inbox. A slogan with an exclamation point—*Free Çilem!*—and beneath it, in capital letters, a phrase in Turkish I don't understand, already more than 100,000 signatures. Just look at that face. Bleached hair, eyebrows thick and black, arched, her expression completely closed, head high, an overall toughness—her face a dare. A police officer on either side of her, she's handcuffed at the wrist. A T-shirt that reads, in English, *Dear past, thanks for all the lessons.* I painstakingly attempt to decipher the argument in Turkish while Sara explains: nine years of domestic violence, this woman tried in vain to get protection from the police and ultimately used the gun that was aimed at her to kill her husband. To the microphone asking her if she regretted it, she responded simply: “Why is it always women who have to die? Men could stand to die a little, too.” Excellent proposition. Sara laughs, this country drives people crazy. Having been intoxicated beforehand doesn’t necessarily mean anything, it might even have served as an advantage. But one is never completely safe from fireworks. In any case, I like the shirt. Especially how Çilem wears it, with this relentless pride that signals utter despair, the act itself. In smaller print just below, we can read the words: *Dear future, I am ready.*

I have a question—I know I'm disturbing him at work, he doesn't answer but instead turns toward me, as always the door is open to my whims despite a subtle, barely perceptible impatience, an early sign of weariness, a look that asks if it's really the time, and I feel this, I do, but since I never know how to stop when I should stop I sit down at the counter. He goes on doing whatever he was in the middle of doing, sorting receipts, it appears, and Anna grabs a cup, do I want a coffee, I nod—in your opinion, if you had to give just one reason, right now, for *why Charlie*, what would you say? You mean, why everyone cared about the *Hebdo* attacks? Yes. Freedom of expression. But that makes no sense, I say how there've been close to a dozen similar incidents that ought to have been even more galvanizing. Such as? Hrant Dink. Who? I can't even say his name right. Hrant Dink, founder of the first bilingual Turkish and Armenian newspaper, *Agos*, the charismatic and indefatigable promoter of peace, assassinated by a nationalist on the street in Istanbul in 2007. Everyone knows Hrant here, they just call him by his first name, which is, for me, so completely impossible to pronounce. He could have been a universal symbol, no? Why didn't the entire world rise up for freedom of expression then? That could have carried greater weight than protesting ISIS; at least Erdoğan, until proven otherwise, is someone we can talk to. Just then he stops, looks over at me, shoots a sarcastic smirk of thanks for having had the bright idea of coming to discuss the comparative merits of *Charlie* and Hrant Dink, ISIS and Erdoğan, during a rush at the bar. And what if, he ventures, you talked about all this with Georgi. He made some tribute for Hrant, I think. What if you did that instead of getting in my way.

Georgi is an artist. I'm not familiar with his work other than the canvas that looms above our bed, an oil-painting-cum-newspaper-collage that depicts Stalin playing violin with a sickle. I don't love the thing, but no one has asked me what I think about the apartment's decor. Georgi is Bulgarian and speaks French okay, English very well, Russian ideologically and Turkish perfectly, all of this in addition to his first language. As far as I know, he does pretty well for himself—very well, even, judging by the amount of time he spends having breakfast on the terraces of Cihangir. It must be said that Turkish breakfast is an institution. Especially when accompanied by cheeses from Van, an Eastern city, the last stop in Turkish territory on the Silk Road. I want to know more about this work made for Hrant Dink. Georgi's at his regular table, talking to a young woman I don't know. He is an incorrigible seducer. Knows how to put himself at the mercy of all women without difficulty, nothing to lose—never hiding, by the way, the fact that he's madly in love with his wife. Why hide it anyway, girls don't care. Quite the contrary, some see it as a challenge, others a sign of honesty—I'm telling you, not one chick out of ten is put off because I'm married. Georgi motions for me to sit down as he simultaneously orders a cup of tea, placing in front of me various dishes of cheese and jam, some cucumber, too. I announce that I've found a new occupation, that I've decided to become interested in the story of Hrant Dink. Obviously he makes me repeat H-rant Din-k, too, and I wonder aloud whether it's not for this stupid reason of the aspirated *h* followed by an unpronounceable *r* that his name hasn't already become known throughout the world. Pardon me for saying this, my dear, but there are names that travel the world without passing through Paris. No, he didn't know him, saw him on TV of course, the man everyone would've loved to have as a friend, big brother, president. He knows the piece about Hrant I'm talking about, but he didn't make it, Erdağ Aksel did. The girl knows who Erdağ Aksel is, one of the signatories to the "I Apologize" campaign, which called for a collective apology for the "Great Catastrophe" in Armenia and demanded an end to state negationism in 2008. A symbolic gesture never before seen on so great a scale, it followed Hrant's assassination and prompted many Turkish intellectuals, writers, and professors to come forward in an attempt to break the taboo that had just claimed yet another life nearly a century after the 1.5 million lost to the Armenian genocide.

Georgi explains to his companion that I've already written one book, a sort of inventory of methods to kill oneself—at this, the girl looks perplexed—then says to me, delighted, so you're going to do the same with us? One big gallery of political assassinations! You know the one who blew himself up with a car bomb in 1993, remember, he asks the girl, who nods yes but says nothing more, Uğur Mumcu. A Kemalist. There's a plaque in Beşiktaş. And the guy who died in front of your place, what was his name? The one who died for a snowball. Georgi snaps his fingers, annoyed that he can't remember, only the name of the sculptor who did the memorial comes to mind. The girl knows the sculptor, and, if I understand correctly, the birdcage at the end of my street is indeed this very memorial. The guy was a journalist and activist, he was at Gezi, by the way. He was having a snowball fight in the street, broke a window, everyone got angry and he was stabbed. He died saying, please let this be a dream. Nuh Köklü! That's his name. I write it down just in case, but then I steer us back to Hrant, to the piece by Erdağ Aksel. Aksel designed the statuette that's presented each year by the International Hrant Dink Foundation to honour activists who have distinguished themselves in the fight for human rights, freedom of expression, dialogue across differences. I'm surprised that a well-established foundation exists, and Georgi says luckily this country is at the very least capable of a little memory, otherwise what would we be, the nightclub of the Middle East and that's it? I nod as if this were an obvious point, then think of the line from Murat Uyurkulak, "If we had no memory, how would fear persist?" Georgi takes my notebook and removes a marker from the big pencil pocket of his cargo pants, then draws an *H* with serifs, the bottom of the letter wider than the top, as if the letter were lying down, and he asks if I know that photograph of Hrant, the one taken just after his assassination, his body on the ground under a white blanket, his feet sticking out. A hole in the sole of his right shoe. Needless to say, the *H* he draws takes the shape of that body on the ground, feet turned inward. The *H* is a piece of metal made to measure, he explains, returning to the statuette by Erdağ Aksel, embedded into a wooden rectangle split in the middle. The *H* holds the piece of wood together and light comes through the crack. Georgi hands me the sketch and there is a pause. It's clear I've killed the breakfast mood. But then he adds, do you remember that girl who did those performances at Gezi, the one who disappeared overnight? She made an installation for Hrant, too. Sentences from his texts traced onto pigmented Anatolian soil. What were the sentences? How do you expect me to remember, what sentences.

At the Muz, I find an envelope with my name on it containing a biography of Hrant Dink, along with a note from Anna, the server: "I had this at my house, thought it might interest you." I take it back to the apartment, though it's been months since I've opened a book. So much new information every day, I'm constantly on the alert, too tense to take the time to read. But here I am, Hrant's close-up portrait before me, his head so big it barely fits on the cover, every pore visible, bushy eyebrows, just a few white strands in his otherwise dark hair, and thin lips that nearly kiss the name of the book's author, Tuba Çandar. I put the book down on the table, walk around the room, smoke a cigarette, prepare some tea. Then I flip through it. The middle insert with photographs, the timeline. Killed by gunshot on January 19, 2007, in front of his newspaper, *Agos,* in Osmanbey, a lively neighbourhood on the European side of Istanbul. Killed by a young nationalist, seventeen years old, who wanted to rid the country of this insolent Armenian, the "enemy of the Turks." Witness reports from the family. "I saw that the street was completely blocked, I got out of the taxi and ran. I thought, I understood, that if he'd just been injured, there wouldn't have been traffic like that," his son reported. I would have preferred to read Hrant's story the same way we tell our own: without knowing where it leads. Not merely waiting for it to end with his body on the pavement of that all-too-familiar boulevard. His own story cut short, it's those of his loved ones that fill the gap and their memories take hold of my hand, arms, throat. The stuttered accumulation of the same scenario, the same meticulous description repeated ten times over of whatever dumb thing someone was doing when the phone rang, when so-and-so came into the room looking sullen—absurd regrets, terrible ironies, denial. I feel some sort of nervous tic in my jaw. Ece Temelkuran recounts the screams of Dink's wife, Rakel: "We trusted you, we stayed in this country. We trusted you! And now this?" "It's *us* who were defeated that day," adds Ece herself, "in the heart of Istanbul, in broad daylight." A witness recounts that Hrant's last words were for his murderer: "Don't do this, son, stop." I don't hear the key turn inside the lock, nor the sound of the door opening, but suddenly I see a figure in the hallway put down his keys, take off his shoes, quickly I try to compose myself but it only makes things worse and when he enters the living room he finds me short of breath, in tears. He stands there, unmoving. I stammer I don't know what, holding the book as if it's an explanation, then throw it on the floor, at his feet, I wish I'd never read that. His gaze is hesitant, hovering somewhere between sympathy and anger. He picks up the book and runs his hand almost tenderly over Hrant's face and the now-damaged cover.

I call Yemliha in Marseille. At this hour I'm not sure if she'll still be at work. The museum gets abysmal reception due to the concrete cage that surrounds the building, basically requiring one to exit onto the outer pathways to hear anything at all. I call anyway, hoping for her sake that she isn't working this late and she picks up right away, her relaxed voice indicating she's alone and not too busy. She says she's just about to leave. I hear her high-heeled footsteps on the passageway and the strong wind rushing through it. Yem, what would you say if I sent you a proposal for an exhibition about an Armenian journalist from Turkey assassinated in Istanbul in 2007? How can I put this—she doesn't slow down—you're joking, right? Given the fact that your job, it seems to me now, is to write books, and this seems to be a better subject for a book than an exhibition, no? And you really think this type of subject, a Christian assassinated by a Muslim, in the current political climate, right before the elections— Believe me, you don't want to give this to a public institution. So yeah, sure, write a book about this Dink guy, that's a good idea. How's Istanbul, otherwise? You seem to be enjoying yourself, as far as I can tell.

She's not wrong. But writing is so stupid, so solitary, you're slouched in front of a computer all day, I don't know how other people concentrate but it takes almost nothing to distract me, there's always something to read or a video to watch or a message to respond to, never any shortage of interruptions. Plus I don't understand how I always end up with the most miserable subjects—I'd rather dance, drink, have sex. "You think it's so easy to write a book? It ruins your life," even Murat Uyurkulak says so. Now I've got Hrant looking out at me from his grave, from the corner of Tuba Çandar's book. I tell Yemliha that I'm going to email her a pitch anyway, just in case. That's exactly right, she quips. Write two hundred pages and cc your editor.

In Kumkapı, the former Armenian neighbourhood in the old city that slopes down to the Sea of Marmara, Hrant Dink's parents lived for a few years in a fisherman's house with their three children. It didn't last. The father was a good man, everyone agrees on this point, but hopeless when it came to money. He spent his days gambling, which plunged the whole family into poverty and the mother into a deep depression. Divorce at that time, 1961, for a family as economically fragile as they were, and from such a conservative background—it was unthinkable, but they did it. The mother simply couldn't keep the children. Financially, psychologically, she couldn't do it. So the father took them, and how long did he last? A few weeks passed before he returned the three brothers—Hrant, the eldest, was seven—with all their belongings to their mother's doorstep and told them to stay there. Meanwhile their mother was on the balcony, shouting down at them to stay with their father. She cried, she begged, and they argued—she on the balcony and he down below—about which of them would have to take care of the kids. And then the kids disappeared. Poof. The younger brothers say it was Hrant who ran away first, that he suddenly sprinted to the end of the street and they followed him. I do not understand how it's possible that three little boys aged four, five, and seven spent three days and three nights on the street, all alone, before the police found them asleep in a fisherman's basket. Three kids, even small ones, inside a fisherman's basket—it's impossible to imagine what kind of basket this could have been. Perhaps the kind that exists only in legends.

What could they have done, left to fend for themselves in this Istanbul neighbourhood, more than fifty years ago? Today there is no shortage of children on the streets; they'd probably go unnoticed. Roma, Syrians. They sell individual tissues with ample professionalism. Sometimes socks. Who even buys socks like that, from a little street vendor? Why not, though, it's worth it, ten pairs for just a few liras. There are children playing music on café terraces. There is one girl we often see with her little sister dressed in pink sequins who must be no older than ten. She plays the accordion and the younger one plays the tambourine—well, you can't really say the little one is *playing* it, but she has a tambourine in her hand and she's cute. In the park, groups of boys hang out among families picnicking in front of the marina. One time, one of us tried to buy a pack of tissues from one of the boys for five liras—the children wouldn't accept any money unless we took a pack, but five liras was too much to pay for a single pack, and the others wouldn't let him pocket the money, then it turned into a fight, then it seemed as though they forgot why they were fighting and carried on just for the fun of it. At the corner of the cobblestone street, there's a little boy who has just learned to walk, and his mother sits on the ground watching him. He's playing with a pizza box bigger than he is.

In Kumkapı, now largely emptied of its Armenian community and replaced by more recent generations of immigrants, I sit down with Ruqia and her sister in a Syrian restaurant, part of a famous family chain from Damascus recently imported to Istanbul inside the luggage of millions of refugees who have come to terms with the idea that they won't be returning home any time soon, and have consequently turned this neighbourhood into a sort of mini-Syria. A young boy comes to show us a basket full of things for sale. He starts chatting with the two of them a little in Arabic, casually, without the slightest hesitation. How does he know they're Syrian if they don't look anything like the women in the neighbourhood? Ruqia asks me what I think a Syrian woman is supposed to look like, and I gesture toward the girls wearing heavy makeup and veils at the tables around us. Ruqia looks vaguely like Audrey Tautou, could pass for French as easily as I could pass for Syrian, if having brown hair is all it takes. The boy looks at me a little sideways, with curiosity; he thinks he's being discreet, but now he's intrigued by the language Ruqia and I are speaking, worried, maybe, that I'll ruin his sale with my mystery jargon. With some nervousness, pointing to me with his finger, he asks, tongue between his teeth making him lisp, *Turkeeeesh*? Ruqia replies in Arabic that I'm French. He's disappointed and a little embarrassed that he hasn't yet learned, as all street kids must, a few phrases in all the languages that might help them approach tourists. She catches him eyeing our meal and offers to share, he doesn't say no, she makes him up a small plate but he doesn't touch it, and finally she understands that he wants to take it away. She wraps it all up with a piece of bread. He gives her a candy cane, she gives him a pound, and now they're even. She sighs. Before, there were no street children where we lived, we never had this. Now look at all these Syrian children who were born here, who will never know a country in which there are not street children.

In Istanbul, fifty years ago and a few streets away, there were already three little Armenians who had just immigrated from Anatolia. Walking back along the waterfront, we stop to watch the fishermen on the rocks, their backs to the imperial palace. When a fish is caught, cats on the lookout rush to claim their share, and the fishermen let them. Perhaps the three Dink brothers—who are said to have been found sleeping in a basket—were also once fed, in the tradition dating back to the Ottoman Empire, by the generosity of fishermen along the Bosphorus.

After lunch, Ruqia and I went to see a fortune teller. The woman was resplendent, she told me she was from Thessaloniki, that she was even related to Atatürk. She reminded me of the Gypsy Girl Mosaic of Zeugma, the ancient relic saved from the waters who is consulted like an oracle, tucked inside the labyrinthine museum in Gaziantep. An unsmiling Mona Lisa, a spellbound Cassandra, as if surprised, or afraid of something she can no longer say: all that remains of the mosaic is her gaze and her hair, no mouth. This fortune teller also had striking eyes, very intense— Anyway, she told me two things: that my future was not in Turkey, and that she saw a very tall man, a man who is precisely six foot one. That's taller than you, isn't it? He breaks into a beautiful smile. Five feet nine. But in all fairness, I don't know if you can really tell the difference between a six and a five, or a one and a nine, looking at coffee grounds. I ask if he believes in this stuff, and he says he can't believe I went in there with Ruqia in the first place, what the hell were we thinking. I say get this, Ruqia went to have her cards read a few years ago, in Syria, and the psychic told her—are you ready—that she would witness the total collapse of her country. He could not be more unimpressed. You know right now anyone could say the same thing to most people in the region without taking too much of a risk.

The balcony scene with the Dink children is so romantic that even if one might doubt the legitimacy of certain details—the younger brothers' memories sometimes seem a little shaky—you want to believe it anyway, and everyone agrees that it came to shape Hrant's character. After three days on the run, the Dink brothers were placed in the Armenian orphanage, where he'd become everybody's big brother, then director of the orphanage itself; it's also where he would meet his wife, Rakel, also a false orphan from Anatolia. But there's something else about the balcony in that story that is deeply troubling, which few people seem to know about, and it's that some years later when Hrant was an adult and a young father, his mother threw herself off the sixth floor of that same house. She killed herself by jumping from the balcony. I say it twice to him, as if to request that this coincidence, if it can be called that, be validated, but I get no response. Just impatience. So what? It's a pretty striking echo, isn't it? A raised eyebrow, heavy silence. What echo? I always wonder what makes suicide such an indomitable taboo, but it's a question to which I must already know the answer since I don't dare insist. To lighten the mood a little, and because he's cutting some fruit for a fruit salad, I go on by saying it's funny, there are a lot more pieces of apple in an apple than pieces of banana in a banana. But now I've stunned him into pure perplexity, and he looks at me like I'm fucking with him. What are you even talking about. I don't know, just thinking out loud. And what are you going to do with Hrant, his mother's suicide, his murder? I shrug. It helps me understand. And it's interesting, in terms of collective memory, there are some works by Turkish artists, like Erdağ Aksel—I take this opportunity to ask if he knows about the performance Georgi mentioned, the text written on pigmented Anatolian soil. You know, the girl who was doing all those conductor moves at Gezi. He shakes his head as if to say yeah but not really. And you think this is good for you, immersing yourself in all this? You really want stories of suicide and murdered journalists? By yourself at your desk for months, doing all this. As Hrant said—I quote him now, not a little proud of calling him by his first name like everyone else—"since I write, I might as well write what's on my mind." In fact, this could almost be a subject for a graphic novel, don't you think? It's all so visual—the basket, the balcony. But now the fruit salad is finished, he picks up a piece of banana and mutters, problems, problems, problems. At the Muz, there are weekly meetings for a satirical newspaper, he knows the whole team, some of the illustrators are really good, by the way. We'll give it some thought, he says, now I just want to watch a movie and go to sleep. Scrolling through the available downloads, he stops to consider a vile romantic comedy with Julia Roberts, I say I hope you're kidding. He clicks his tongue in annoyance, and I ask if we can instead watch Fatih Akın's film on the Armenian genocide, apparently the first person to die in the film is named Hrant, and he just goes no, no, no.

I feel a distance settle in between us. Snags of silence, moments in which he leaves a conversation hanging to lose himself in his thoughts, which are, to me, increasingly opaque. Not to mention a minor detail: we've stopped having sex. I've tried candlelit dinners, dressed up, what is this nonsense, are we celebrating Valentine's Day now? Leave the candles alone, we need them for the power cuts. I say how Valentine's Day must have been invented so couples like us could make love at least once a year. He rolls his eyes, a little amused. I wonder if it's all my fault, but this annoys him. It's not me, the world doesn't revolve around me, and if I start putting pressure on him, nothing's going to get any better. Okay. Would it be easier if I were Turkish? Sara the psychologist (who had already warned me about the counterproductive nature of this kind of confrontation) says that it's becoming more and more common among men here, a sort of national depression, anxiety on the rise since the last elections, or since the collapse of the restorative spirit that energized Gezi—there are some who've gone months or years with no libido. What does it mean to be Turkish—you think the 50 percent who vote for Erdoğan and the 10 percent who vote for fascists *also* suffer this national depression? You're neither more nor less Turkish than I am, it doesn't mean anything, nothing at all, *being Turkish* is not a thing. And actually, I'm increasingly in the minority in thinking this, so *you* can't start now. Still, it's becoming a joke, foreigners are thinning out, expats are leaving, and fewer and fewer new ones are coming to take their place. So it's in the midst of all this that I'm being asked, more than ever, what it is I'm doing here. Beckett: "We don't travel, as far as I know, for the pleasure of travelling. We're dumb, but not that dumb." Especially to a country that bears a slight resemblance to the *Titanic*. The city scowls and its residents are losing their sheen. It seems our charm doesn't work on Istanbul anymore, he says, a theory that leaves me stunned and him pensive, as he mindlessly flicks a piece of crumbling plaster off the balcony. Nor does our optimism, obviously.

How reasonable is it to try to hold on to what we have here? The Muz is once again being threatened with administrative closure. Someone has to go negotiate with the municipality to get them to leave the Muz alone and he's the one to take on the task, albeit with little hope that the authorities will act in good faith. A few months ago, they shut down all the businesses in the neighbouring alley—tea vendors, a jeweller, a bookstore—under the pretext that they didn't have licences for selling alcohol. But no one was selling alcohol. And this wasn't enough to fix anything—everything remained closed and the shopkeepers became discouraged and then a miracle, a real estate developer showed up, bought the passageway, and now there are plans to open a luxury hotel for wealthy tourists from the Gulf region. It's obvious that the meetups of leftist artists at the Muz are not part of the city council's urban development plan. He looks good, he's wearing his nice shoes and a long-sleeved shirt to hide his tattoos. I'm going to the police station and then I'm going straight to work, don't wait up for me later. He's working night shifts with increasing frequency, at his own request, I think. Or simply because the others don't want to anymore, they get too bored staying so late, with only the core group of founders left to keep the place going. But how long's it been since we last went out for dinner? We used to be so friendly with the owners of the meze restaurant, and now they must think we've moved. And looking at the leftovers of our quick, bare-bones meals—it's painful to take in. He clears the plates, stacks the glasses, the teacups, cutlery; his movements as he does this are decisive, confident, then he brings everything into the kitchen, rests the stack on the side of the sink, runs the water. The water comes out in loud copper-coloured spurts. There must be something in the pipes. He stands there for what begins to feel like too long, watching the murky water run without improvement, as if dumbstruck. He sighs, fucking third world. He turns off the tap and hurls the pile of dishes across the kitchen, everything crashes to the floor in the corner in one loud smash of glass. I watch him as he grabs his jacket and leaves, slamming the door behind him.

I don't know if he came back that night, if he slept, maybe not, maybe on the couch. When I wake up I hear sounds of glass being swept up in the kitchen. He pokes his head into the bedroom and says be careful, he's dressed to go out for a run, and nodding toward the kitchen he says he's put everything in the corner and then he gestures toward the corner with the smile of an embarrassed little boy, it seems we're a thousand miles away from yesterday's mood, don't go into the kitchen barefoot, to which I say yes, father, and with a genuine smile this time he takes a chair to block the entrance to the kitchen, as if I were going to disobey, as if that'd be capable of stopping me, and comes back to repeat once more for me to be careful, he'll clean it all up later but right now he's going to get some sun, it's a beautiful day. When I get up I go into the kitchen and look down at the pile of broken glass. I feel almost as if it's challenging me, like it's going to stay there for a long time, longer than me, maybe.

"For no particular reason, just a little discouraged." This is the sentence on the canvas that hangs in Jean's entrance. In 1980—you weren't even born yet—I had just published the book that caused such a scandal, and a painter friend called me to ask how I was feeling, and I said, without any particular reason, just a little discouraged. He laughed, and a few weeks later I received this painting. Jean identifies as an old Armenian with equal parts regret and pride. Hrant, who never got to see him old, called him the Armenian of Marseille, "a madman like me," he'd say. Jean asks about my Turkish lover and cuts short my Pandora-like grievances to grumble, well, if I were forty years younger I'd have suggested you swap him out for an Armenian, but now, what can I offer you? A whisky? I accept. This is a provocation, or a test, the morning whisky, but I'm no stranger to this game. He's not surprised by my interest in Hrant. Etyen Mahçupyan, who succeeded Hrant as head of *Agos*, once said it's hard to be indifferent to the warmth of that voice, "difficult not to feel how much this man struggled to seek and find humanity, fumbling as if blindfolded in a game of blind man's bluff." People like him, Jean adds, are rare, each generation gets only one, if that. He was an exceptional person. Obviously that's why he was killed. I tell him I'm reading the biography by Tuba Çandar. Jean doesn't seem to know about it, which is surprising given that he's quoted at length in it. Oh yeah? What'd I say? My father's orphanage, is that it?

No. What does your father's orphanage have to do with it? Jean says, as if everyone already knew this, that his father, a survivor of the genocide, stayed at the Armenian orphanage in Şişli, Istanbul, before leaving Turkey for good and moving to Marseille. When, in the early 2000s, Jean made the return journey from Marseille and landed in Istanbul, following in his parents' footsteps, it was only natural that he sought out Hrant for advice—*Agos* was the window to the Armenian community in Turkey—and it was with him that he visited the orphanage. He served as an interpreter for my interviews, Jean says, because I speak neither Turkish nor English. I'm surprised. But yeah, he was such a helpful person. Which I don't doubt, but he spoke French? Jean looks at me as if I were a lost cause. They were speaking Armenian, of course, and I'm officially a moron. Because I seem to be stuck at square one, I take this opportunity to ask some basic questions, like what does the name of the newspaper, *Agos*, mean? Jean makes a gesture of sowing seeds by the fistful. *Agos* means *The Furrow*. It was a word shared by Turks and Armenians; at least by the peasants, back when they lived together. The furrow—like in "The Marseillaise?" *Let blood impure / water our furrows*—ironic, for someone murdered by a nationalist. Jean nods, if you're looking for prophecies with Hrant, you won't be disappointed. During a conference to which Hrant had been invited to talk about minorities in Turkey, one of the speakers, a Kurd, had thought it useful to note that Turks and Kurds had fought together, and Hrant responded: "What peace are we even talking about, if we base our brotherhood on blood we have shed together? Don't you think I'll ask you whose blood it was you shed?"

Jean doesn't open up easily and often loses his train of thought, so I try not to interrupt him. But still, maybe he knows that artist who did a performance based on a text, from what I understand, traced on pigmented Anatolian soil. This was a good call. He rises to get a book in his beautifully arranged bookcase, an exhibition catalogue from the gallery next to the Muz—it's crazy how you sometimes have to embark upon these massively convoluted detours only to find what you were looking for on your doorstep. She's exactly my age. And here are the photos of this patch of red earth, on which she's traced a dozen barely legible lines in Turkish. The catalogue is translated only into Armenian, so the old Armenian translates it into French for me, with his Marseille accent. It's a response to the arguments of those who don't want to recognize the genocide because they fear that the descendants of the victims will ask for compensation. "Yes, it's true, Armenians have their eyes fixed on this land of our roots. They don't look away, but it's not so they can re-conquer it. Deep down, they want to be buried there." Jean adds with sadness in his voice that Hrant wanted, more than anything in the world, not to be forced to leave his country, and at least his wish was granted: his impure blood did eventually water the land of his ancestors. As the Armenian proverb goes, the water finally found its crack.

Language is an increasingly frustrating deficiency. I continue to work on my Turkish lessons but get stuck on the chapter about indirect speech. Everything gets complicated—who's talking to whom, who's there, who's not there. Most of the time, you simply repeat the words you hear, a verb sprinkled here and there to signal that you're quoting, and that's it. I try to practise some phrases, at least when writing banal, everyday messages, and their usual recipient invariably welcomes them with amused kindness but doesn't encourage me to start speaking aloud either. Obviously we're more comfortable in English, and the fact that we are both communicating in a second language seems, to him, more egalitarian. He's used to it, having had pretty much exclusively foreign girlfriends, a pattern that is astonishingly common in our circle. Mixed couples are the norm among our friends. It's a way of opening up to the world, isn't it? He sees I'm unsatisfied with such a platitudinous answer so he gives up and sighs, if you want to know the truth, I just don't like to make love in my mother tongue. This confession, which I almost immediately report to Sara, makes her swoon. She advises me to instead write a book about the psychology of men from Turkey, I'd have more success and a lot less trouble than bothering with Hrant—but then again, both entities would probably benefit from being better understood.

You can hear that he speaks other languages. There is no shortage of French words in Turkish, but the other day he learned a new one: *beauf*, which he immediately starts using to describe nationalist kids with their shaved heads and pseudo-virile moustaches. He pronounces the word *boof* and asks why we don't write *buff* instead; when I explain to him where the word comes from, he wonders whether it's really all that reasonable to have incorporated, like a palimpsest, various indecipherable etymological roots into the spelling of words. He sighs at the idea that we use a specific *i* and *f* for Greek words and that there is *also* an exception to this exception for the Arabic word for water lily, *nenuphar*. Conversely, Turkish is written just how it sounds, regardless of the origin of words that spring up as if out of nowhere. This is an example of the frenzied assimilation that makes one wonder why France does not practise it, as our two countries often find themselves on the same page when it comes to linguistic nationalism. In Turkey, debates about minority languages are ongoing without resolution, even though twenty years ago Hrant wrote that he was "claiming [his] share of the Kurdish language." He had married an Armenian woman from Turkey whose mother tongue was Kurdish, and thus demanded the right to enroll his children in Kurdish-speaking schools, just as non-Armenians should have the right to enroll their children in Armenian schools. "What is right for these lands," he said, with the simplicity of common sense shining through this imbroglio, "is the coexistence of differences." And as if that weren't enough, he'd also put his foot in it with Islam, with his typical optimism and freely Voltairean accents: "It is much more fruitful for different religions to live together, with each other, rather than apart. For if we manage to correctly interpret differences, we may realize that they nourish, not destroy, each other. The muezzin's call to prayer, heard five times a day by a Christian like me"—for Hrant was as much a Christian as an atheist, he was Christian *and* atheist—"reminds him that he is Christian." If we are to assume that hatred comes from fear, and fear comes from ignorance of the other, then all we need is education to live happily together, deeply fulfilled, forever and ever, amen.

These incantations about coexistence, which were written in 2005, strike me as a spectacularly failed recipe. But perhaps like Saint Euphemia, torn apart by lions seventeen centuries ago, Hrant's words—strewn throughout books translated into all the languages, haunting us, outliving their messenger, present in Turkish, Kurdish, Armenian memory, and now our memory, too—might still work a miracle, however delayed.

For once, without pause, without silence, without reserve, he erupts as he speeds ahead, shooting off loud insults about the indecency of these idiot governments and railing against the agreement between Turkey and the European Union. What's this business of exchanging visas for refugees, where are we now—in what century, what democracy? Turkey is wearing him down but Europe is worse, a disappointment, a total abandonment. I thought the idea of the EU was to avoid a third world war, but clearly not. Duly noted. This agreement allocates billions to the Turkish state, with the added bonus—which no one really believes in, and Erdoğan will always take the opportunity to seize the baton of broken promises when it suits him—of a commitment to abolish Schengen entry visas for Turkish citizens. In exchange for what? No guarantees of human rights, of course—no, what really interests the richest countries in the world of the twenty-first century is that the refugees arriving from Syria, already more than three million on this side of the border, go no further. And we just wash our hands of these catastrophically predictable conditions and the consequences of an already unstable situation. Aslı Erdoğan writes, "Europe must take responsibility by returning to the values it defined, after centuries of bloodshed, values that make 'Europe Europe': democracy, human rights, freedom of expression." This appeal has gone unanswered. My neighbour Metin is a journalist and is rather skeptical about the good intentions of the U.S. He grimaces at the idea of calling on Europe for help, suspicious of unwelcomed paternalism and critical of what he considers a way for Turks to avoid taking responsibility for their own failures. Hrant, who was equally disillusioned, had no qualms about calling out imperial powers: "If Europe had truly behaved responsibly, would we ultimately have experienced these painful times, all this collapse?" At the same time he mocked the semblance of good conscience that the French and German parliaments bought themselves by recognizing the Armenian genocide, and said that Europe's debt was undeniable: "We must admit that the interest shown in the past for this region of the world by a divided Europe has led to the exhaustion of its peoples." Here I suspect a translation problem. I wonder aloud if one can really *exhaust* someone by showing them interest, but his answer, without hesitation, is: duh.

I nod vaguely in agreement without adding anything else, not worth it to continue, and anyway now I'm looking for my lighter at the bottom of my bag, no doubt lost among the thousand useless things I carry around—though it must be said that between a phone, a dozen pens, and a tube of lipstick, one could surely start a fire—and I run straight into a little pile of cat food placed carefully on the edge of the sidewalk. This irritates him; I go *oops* and try to rebuild the pile because you don't mess around with street cats here. I continue digging in my bag as I cross the street a little dangerously, a scooter swerves to avoid me, and it is at this moment that an elderly man with a grey beard who is sitting on a little stool with his tea gets up and walks straight toward me, sticks a lighter under my nose, its flame already lit, and says, ceremoniously, with a huge grin: *Madame*. I jump and barely manage to suppress an aggressive,

Parisian reflex that nearly has me lash out at this poor man who is looking me in the eyes with his lighter held out, a simple, kind gesture. I light my cigarette and thank him with all the polite phrases I know in Turkish as he turns to my companion, who is eyeing us with slight dismay. The old man puts his hand on his chest to convey his good faith and apologizes for scaring me. The other reaches a protective arm around me and grabs my hand as if I were four years old. "And here we are standing now, my country and I, hair in the wind, my hand puny in its enormous fist"—I like the echo of this Césaire poem as something to follow this morning's anger.

During Gezi, a historian took photos of the banners hanging on the Atatürk Cultural Centre. Despite the excitement and euphoria of the moment, he felt that very few people would bear witness to what was written there once the trap door closed. He said we'd do well to be wary, already reading in 2013 in the Western press that Turkish democracy was in full regression. But perhaps it was one step ahead. Hrant said nothing else, despite his unyielding optimism. He wrote that "while European Christians are just beginning to adapt, as best they can, to a multicultural way of life that includes Muslims and Armenians, they, like other Eastern Christians (Syriac, Chaldean, etc.), [have] experienced both the positive and negative aspects of this reality. Today they are the custodians of an invaluable experience. [...] Improving upon what was done well in the past, not repeating what was done badly. Now that's a lesson for Europe." Jean Kéhayan, the Armenian of Marseille, adds to this in his own writing: "If Turkey refused to begin the process of joining the European Union, it would be crucial that the founding nations of Europe deploy their diplomatic skills to convince Ankara to take this step." But on both sides, the desire for reconciliation was fragile, a minority position, motivated on the European side largely by the fear that an unstable Turkey would be more dangerous outside than inside—and fear rarely leads to true reconciliation, right? Hrant had hoped to transform European cynicism into a genuine interest in what this place had to offer: "We must remember Anatolia a hundred years ago: wouldn't Europe be begging for this country?"

But that isn't what his contemporaries chose to remember. "Love it or leave it"—Sarkozy dug up this refrain to fuel his 2007 campaign, promising his voters that he'd slam the door on Muslim Turkey's entry into Europe once and for all. These words were once chanted through the windows of *Agos* during the demonstrations that preceded Hrant's assassination. It was in service to this ridiculous principle of having to love one's country no matter what that Hrant was persecuted, in three separate trials, for insulting Turkish national identity. Besides, this law that punishes people who don't love their country in the exact way they're told to love it—I'd be surprised if you didn't inherit it soon, the way democracy's looking in your country. When you consider the fact that it was in hopes of getting rid of these tribal laws that Hrant pushed for integration into the EU, we'd hardly be surprised if one of the countries in the Union in turn adopted a law repressing blasphemy, even if it were republican.

But let's give Europe the credit it deserves: it knows a thing or two about symbols. The kind that arrive too late to be useful but that comfort the few survivors that remain by giving them, if not the feeling that justice has finally been achieved, at least the hope that what happened to them will not happen again. "I am filing an appeal with the European Court of Human Rights," Hrant wrote in the article published the day he died. "I don't know how many more years this will last. What I do know, and what reassures me somewhat, is that until the end of the trial, I will continue living in Turkey. If the Court rules in my favour, it means I will never be forced to leave my country, and this would be my greatest happiness." The ECHR ultimately ruled post-mortem on this critical case for freedom of expression. Therefore, in 2010, nearly four years after Hrant's death, the Turkish state was convicted in the case of "Dink v. Turkey." Europe referred to Dink using his Turkified first name, Fırat; the irony behind their denial of his Turkish identity clearly went unnoticed.

These were the conclusions of Judges Sajó and Tsotsoria: "It is possible that a number of people felt so outraged by Fırat Dink's writings that they decided to kill him, but this cannot be a relevant consideration. The authorities should have prevented the murder. It would be the end of all freedom of expression and democracy if the authorities of a country were allowed to silence those who express themselves publicly simply by refusing to allocate resources to the maintenance of public order and security. Outrage, even if it stems from specific remarks, is not in itself a factor of violence, and we cannot blame authors for potential unrest in cases where the alleged unrest actually originates from the unhappiness of those to whom the remarks were addressed. To understand that the outrage, disturbance, or riots that might result from them constitutes a legitimate reason to limit freedom of expression would be tantamount to granting a right of veto to troublemakers, allowing violent groups who disagree with someone to exercise their own *freedom of expression* by imposing their view of acceptable speech onto that person."

Hrant, in one of his last published pieces, writes that while nationalists marched beneath his windows to lay funeral wreaths, chanting, "Love us or leave us," he was summoned to appear before the Istanbul court. The prosecutor warned him of all the possible consequences of his writings, as did the police chief, who nevertheless did not see fit to protect him. "Don't you think you should act with more caution? Do you realize the extent of the pandemonium you've caused? As you surely must know, the streets are filled with all kinds of fanatics," and so on. Shortly after that, in France, *Charlie Hebdo* republished Danish cartoons of Muhammed. Jacques Chirac, then president of the Republic, officially condemned "all obvious provocations likely to dangerously stir up emotions," while Minister of the Interior Nicolas Sarkozy droned on about how Turkey was definitely *not like us*.

Of course there are double standards, Fares snaps. We've carried our conversation into the Muz and Fares has picked up a bit of it as he tries, his face crunched into a scowl, to get the coffee maker to work. Fares hasn't been in Istanbul long, nor does he intend to spend the rest of his life making coffee. Just a few months ago he was a dentist in Aleppo. And then he ended up in Istanbul, I'm not sure how, and his partner, the beautiful Anna, has joined him here. Anna is Ukrainian. She doesn't have a residence permit in Turkey. She makes coffee all day long without complaining, but not Fares. He speaks English, French, and already a little Turkish—more than I do, though I've been here much longer. He knows how to do everything except make a cappuccino. He stops and stands in front of me. What surprises you? France produces content and spreads it across the world—everything that's happening in your country is broadcast automatically, as if on a highway lined with speakers. Just look at Naji Jerf, who was assassinated just after *Hebdo*; he was the best guy in the world, a journalist, an excellent filmmaker, committed to the fight against Assad and ISIS (he doesn't say Daesh, no one says Daesh here, everyone prefers to use ISIS, the Islamic State in Iraq and Syria—or the Levant, ISIL). Except you didn't see people rushing to buy his newspaper when he was shot. No one bothered to translate *Hentah* into ten different languages to show the world which media outlet had just been decapitated. I'd be surprised if a single television network broadcast his documentary in the name of freedom of expression, yet it was precisely because of this film that he was murdered. I guess it's only ISIS who bother to watch the work of journalists in the field, who think the work is so important and potentially harmful that they shoot the journalists dead.

I type "Naji Jerf" into YouTube. "ISIL in Aleppo," a twenty-six-minute documentary in Arabic. Posted by Naji on December 15, 2015, two weeks before his assassination. 76,976 views. A long scene in which we see a mother, wearing a chador and gloves, pleading to ISIS jailers to release her son, defending herself against accusations that she comes from a progressive family. But go find out for yourselves, our family is not secular, my son can't be accused of that. She begs, but it's too late. Her son has been executed. The guard washes his hands of it, not his fault. Naji's YouTube account has been around since 2011, and there are some other, older videos of an oud player in a red-lit room with white floor tiles. The musician looks Kurdish; he sings for a small audience, we hear the voice of a woman speaking to him, some applause, he laughs. The camera is steady, probably a small one on a tripod. Naji didn't bother to name the video and uploaded it onto YouTube with its original file name, MVI 9327, followed by a second video entitled MVI 9328, which contains the rest of the concert. Posted on December 28, 2014, the first day of the last year of his life that would end the following December 27. 446 views. A single comment, which starts off okay: "On Sunday the 27th of December in 2015, the brave Syrian journalist and maker of acclaimed documentaries about the heinous crimes perpetrated against the defenceless Syrian people, and against other defenceless peoples in the Near & Middle

East by the merciless mercenary armies called ISIS"—and then the hatch opens—"(ISIS = IsraHell Secret Intelligence Service)..." No need to read any further—I know all too well conspiracy theorists' rambling diatribes and bad puns, which, with what little wit they possess, never fail to bring everything, always, back to Israel.

I wonder how Naji would engage with these kinds of comments on his page. Would he respond to them, would he delete them. I click on his photo, as if to read an answer into his intense gaze, which is turned toward something else. This encounter with his face overwhelms me—his striking resemblance to the man who, just a few inches from me, is rolling a cigarette. Can I show you something? I turn the screen a little. It's like showing him a mirror. Naji Jerf is his doppelgänger, just barely older. There are a few front-facing portraits in which he looks straight at the camera with pride, warmth, seriousness. And then some other photos with children, two pretty young girls he's holding in his arms. I think back to election night last year, when Erdoğan's AK Party passed the absolute majority threshold in Parliament, and you said sadly, like you were giving up, how you'd have to be completely twisted to have children in this country now. He looks pained. He asks what's wrong with me.

Anna grabs our coffees and motions for me to follow her, we go outside to sit on the benches in the back, in the employees' smoking area, an open space built on the ruins of a collapsed building that overlooks the street behind, surrounded by lemon trees whose pots double as ashtrays. On the floor above, loud music emanates from the balcony of a tattoo shop all day long. On the other side of the ruin that serves as our courtyard—and for the kittens, a playground—another shop is setting up what appears to be a winter lounge. Erol, once a biker, now a small shopkeeper out of necessity, is mounting some shelves outside, like a little library. Anna and I sit next to the lemon trees, he waves and invites us to have some tea, but Anna doesn't move and looks a little lost. Fares doesn't want children either, he says that given their situation it's out of the question. And it's true that they're both undocumented, living in a miserable apartment so small that a morning shower gets the whole place wet, plus the unconquerable cockroaches, and they both work ten hours a day, six days a week, with no holidays, all for 1,200 liras per month, while housing prices in the neighbourhood are listed in dollars. Anna knows all this, just as she knows she's at an age where it's now or never. She smiles like she always does, with the laugh of a little girl who apologizes because she knows she's an adult. She can't help saying it: she hates what's happening to her, it's horrible to grow old without children, don't you think? I tell her that life seems infinitely simpler to me that way. But you, she said, you could—she casts a glance inside the café—I mean, not here, not with him. It irritates me when people tell me what to do, especially when it's always the exact same thing. Anna, you could leave, too, you have a passport, why are you still here? No more apologetic giggles. But I'm like you, my dear. I'm waiting for the fireworks.

He's sleeping. Stretched out on the couch, in a ray of setting sunlight. I lean over him and he winks, puts his hand on my stomach. I sit down as gently as possible.

Do you know how you can recognize dominant animals in the savannah? They don't jump when they wake up. He smiles, that's right, and you're some kind of kamikaze gazelle. He feels my ribs, have you eaten? I nod yes, though it's not true. It's as if I have something caught in my eye that can't be blinked away, whether my eyes are open or closed, it's there, Naji Jerf, his name whistles in my ears, his face flickers before my eyes. The missing image: Naji murdered, a bullet fired from a silencer in the middle of the street in Gaziantep; his body fallen, then disconnected, then dead.

These aren't my words, but Amin Maalouf's, back in 2004: "The unrest in Turkey is *intense*. The country turned its back on its Ottoman past and gave up its primacy within the Muslim world in order to identify with Europe, meanwhile Europe continues to dwell in the memory of the Janissaries beneath the walls of Vienna. What do you do when you have an abyss behind you and a closed door, or a door that's just barely open, in front of you?" For once I wake up early, but I'm alone in the apartment and don't want to face this rainy, ugly, miserable morning for anything in the world. I run a bath. I balance my computer on the edge of the towel rack and put on a French radio station. It's Saturday morning in Istanbul, and I have Alain Finkielkraut in my bathroom. I need hot water to relax a little. Lately I've been remembering my dreams, and they've been almost totally incomprehensible. Last night I dreamed I was pulling carrots out of the ground. Were the carrots a little oversized, or was it me who had shrunk? I pulled them out quite easily, in fact, from a vegetable garden path where they were sticking out too far and getting in my way and my arms were full of carrots and I didn't know what to do with them. Something's vibrating. I twist out of the tub to grab my phone from the edge of the sink. A message from Elsa. Is everything okay? I don't like this question. No, I don't like it one bit. I check online for breaking news: explosion on İstiklal, number of victims still unknown. The Muz is right next door. It's Saturday morning so it's probably empty, but I have to call just to make sure. It's probably, very probably, closed. Which also doesn't mean there's no one there. But do I need to get out of the bathtub. I decide to stick my head underwater and count to ten before calling. That should be fine. One, two, ten. He answers right away, he was at the market, everything's okay. I can't really believe this was an attack, he says, you'd have to be an idiot to blow yourself up on a Saturday morning in İstiklal. It's the heart of the city, and one is usually forced to move at a snail's pace amid a throng of people, an inevitable pedestrian traffic jam beginning every day at noon, packed in and around stores, restaurants, bars—but in the morning, especially on a Saturday, it's dead. Or it's the PKK, he continues, it wasn't far from the police station, that could have been a target. In any case he tells me not to get too upset, none of our friends are likely to have been awake and outside so early in the morning. I hang up, I don't like this calm that rings false, too rational, as if it were normal to call *just in case*. I remain motionless in the water, trying to find a way to expel the alarm that has begun to creep into my body. I wish I could let the water run and drench the bathroom, wash over the entire apartment, flow all the way down the stairs. Not technically feasible, I admit. While people are blowing themselves up and others are dying in the streets, the Saturday-morning bath is undisturbed. Same goes for Finkielkraut, who hasn't stopped yapping. Still holding my phone, I dip it gently, and with some cruelty, into the water. And then that's enough, I get out of the bathtub and leave the phone to soak.

My ears are ringing, I don't know what's stopping me from cutting them off. What time is the next yoga class, I need to hurry, I grab my things and slam the door and I've forgotten my keys inside but whatever. I wait for the ferry with music blaring from my earbuds to drown out the noise and think about something else—to try not to suspect any of my neighbours of carrying explosives because they seek and wish to carry out the total destruction of all humanity, above all to try not to imagine it and to concentrate very hard on containing this fear during the crossing, without so much as a glance into the deep waters of the Bosphorus. I climb the steep hill of Cihangir at full speed up to the yoga studio. I join the class, which has already begun, and I am temporarily stilled, calm, just one girl who is slightly too thin among others inside the Zen ambience of Istanbul's hipsters. How I ended up here, having to focus on my breathing in Turkish so as not to be destroyed by total fear of the world—it's something I can't think about.

As I leave, I sense the presence of worried messages swirling around me like ghosts, messages asking if I'm at the apartment, saying that he came back and I wasn't there, that he found my phone drowned in the bathtub and doesn't know how to get in touch with me, where am I, how am I, messages ordering me to get home. I feel like I need to walk, and walk a lot, it's early evening now. I could cross the Bosphorus by foot if only someone would part the waters for me. I try to recite lines from the little book by Aslı Erdoğan that so beautifully recounts her nighttime wanderings in Geneva, *The Miraculous Mandarin.* She writes: "Every night, without fail, I walk the streets [...] like the ghost of a woman who died in the previous century. It was only there, in that ancient city full of memories, of old, imposing, soulless buildings, and also of dreams and ghosts, that my interior universe, completely crowded with ruins, could find refuge." I wonder to myself if Aslı, the flâneuse of Istanbul, is still in exile, if right now she's wandering some European city as I roam hers. I didn't know, thinking about her that night, that I was just a few blocks away from her apartment, that the police would soon come to take her away. If I passed her that evening I couldn't have known it, wouldn't have recognized her.

Before I get too lost in Şişli, I find my way back to Erdem's place and ring the doorbell; it's already late and I don't want to go home. He unfolds the sofa bed without protest, saying that to gain perspective you need time, to go to the old city, to Constantinople, all the way to Byzantium if necessary, we can go there together tomorrow if I want. Sometimes I try to recapture the sense of astonishment I felt the first few times I was there, standing in front of Hagia Sophia, but to no avail: since the attacks on the Blue Mosque, the esplanade where we used to sit has become completely militarized. If I sat on the terraces above like before, I'd feel like Nero. Erdem and I venture a little further past the tourist area and into the old Armenian quarter, now largely Islamized with freshly repainted mosques amid dilapidated buildings. Here you can still make out a bell tower colonized by ivy, the rest of the church inaccessible, even the entrance is walled up. And over there, a fountain and star-shaped alleys lined with fish restaurants that have added terraces and rooftop seating to offer a glimpse of the Sea of Marmara above the neighbourhood's general congestion. Over the past few years, a new trend has emerged, the busiest streets have bloomed into a forest of colourful umbrellas, three or four metres above the ground. These umbrellas have replaced the vine trellises that, judging by their omnipresence on the ruins of abandoned buildings, must have previously provided shade to shoe vendors sitting on the sidewalks, right in front of stores that now sell the same shoes at double the price. Just like the traffic on the streets parallel to the waterfront, the tea rooms and kebab shops are crowded with people. Almost all of them are men, the older ones sitting down, the younger ones in groups on the street. The way I look, the way I'm dressed—sleeveless, sunglasses, the canvas tote that serves as my handbag—and despite my dark hair, Erdem and I do not go unnoticed. By contagion, people speak to him in English, too, sometimes even directly in French. The Istanbul shopkeepers have a knack for guessing where you're from, and Erdem seems a little surprised before noticing the name of the Parisian bookstore emblazoned on my tote bag. You could at least make an effort to be a little discreet. What, you want me to wear a T-shirt that says Nâzim Hikmet?—the poet and communist martyr who has become a Che Guevara–like icon. Erdem nods and at the same time concedes that it's not guaranteed to be any better received in this neighbourhood. In a shop that sells counterfeits, we find a tote bag with the Muz's slogan, written in English: *They call it chaos, we call it home.* I buy it. We walk down the narrow streets to the Armenian episcopate, which is sandwiched between two police stations, like fixed checkpoints. Opposite is the glorious church with its blue and pink interior and soft lighting. A mother and child pass us, and Erdem asks if I can identify the language they are speaking, where they come from; I'd say West Africa. Indeed, there they are, the new minority of the city. "But they don't have, so to speak, the consistency of old figures, now disappeared and already almost imperceptible—Armenians, Greeks, Jews, even the Syriacs. Those figures truly represented the essence of Istanbul, both Byzantium and the capital of the

Ottoman Empire." Erdem loves poetry and has a fondness for translation. I ask him to tell me more about it as we walk up, down, then zigzag across the streets, my sense of direction increasingly jumbled. Another church completely enclosed within its narrow walls. Gedikpaşa: the street of the orphanage where Hrant Dink and his brothers spent their childhood. We climb as they must have climbed so many times, surely prancing more lightly, with more energy than us, up and down these secular cobblestones. For years the Dink children, although placed in the orphanage, would visit their mother every day, serving as her couriers in town to deliver her sewing work to clients, thanks to which she survived, albeit meagrely. You can imagine the devotion of these children, who had only this one connection to their mother. Solemnly Erdem recites, to the rhythm of his steps, a poem of inexpressible sadness, "Tragedies" by Edip Cansever:

We are stuck inside a very dark sentence
Stuck inside a sentence
In which everyone, absolutely everyone, roams
In which all the letters, all the lines
Are endlessly missing each other

The orphanage and school are at the front of a church that is charmless but still in use. Today—it's Sunday—religious songs and children's laughter escape from it. In the courtyard, more children are playing. I enter the building quietly, so as not to interrupt the service. Some women encourage me to join them, but I stop at a table with books and Bibles and notice a beautiful edition of psalms in Armenian. I take it. Behind me, in the parking lot, men are talking and smoking near the street vendors who criss-cross the tourist district during the week. These red carts sell small round sesame seed rolls. When I take the boat from one side of the city to the other, I always buy one to share with the seagulls that follow the ferry.

We take a break at the top of the hill to catch our breath, turn around, and notice that we're high enough to see the Sea of Marmara at the end of the street. You don't see the Bosphorus on this side, and the horizon opens onto the sea, with no opposite shore. Nowhere to go. The uncertain water into which migrants throw themselves every night, departing from the southern Turkish beaches. A cargo ship passes slowly through the narrow frame. Behind it, we see dozens more lined up, awaiting the green light to enter the strait. It's like a game of battleship. An old man sits down next to us on a stool to feed the pigeons. Erdem asks me if I know the poetry of İlhan Berk, his collection called *St. Antoine's Pigeons.* I shake my head no. What follows is like an incantation.

For now Lambodis have nothing to fear
Eleni has nothing to fear
The pigeons will all take flight and no one will know fear
An hour when everything wakes
Love will begin
Everything will stop

Hrant, in his last published text, compared himself to a fearful pigeon, living in fear, on the lookout for anyone who might throw the first stone. He also noted, as if to reassure himself, what he knew about this country, which is that no one hurts the birds. Erdem and I walk down the coast and, bypassing the crowds, head toward the mosque known as Little Hagia Sophia. It's lovely here, with its garden, gazebo, and the frolicking, somewhat improbable animals—cats, of course, but also rabbits and ducks. The old man who serves tea in the garden recognizes me; sometimes I come here to do little more than watch those who come and go at prayer time. One man washes his hands slowly, another sets out a little bowl of water for the cats. I could spend hours observing the self-contained life of this garden, a sacred bubble in this neighbourhood that has become otherwise dulled by mass tourism. I identify quite a bit with the fat white rabbit, who seems to rely on the cats' benevolent protection of the garden so it can graze in peace. The ducks are almost cutthroat by contrast and often end up being chased off by the children. We are served tea, I'm still holding my book of psalms. Unlike my sparse general knowledge and wayward movements through hybrid and poetic works, Erdem's formidable memory allows him to recite all kinds of texts, including religious ones. He regrets not having learned Arabic, but when he was growing up, when people had the opportunity to learn languages and travel, they learned French and went to Europe. I say Arabic for practical reasons, he says, but I would have liked to have immersed myself in Persian, which permeates Turkish language and culture, and would have been this whole other opening into our world. Do you realize that here the call to prayer is in Arabic, and no one understands it—except the refugees, of course, and our new friends from the Emirates. And on the graves of our Ottoman ancestors, even reading the names is impossible. Atatürk made a big move, changing the alphabet to Latin pretty much overnight—the only thing more radical is Israel and its resurrection of Hebrew.

I like Hebrew, its unusual, timeless script, which for me embodies a sort of literary essence. Erdem laughs, yes, Hebrew is very powerful—a language that has fascists, leftists, and Islamists against it must not be underestimated. The Armenian alphabet is similar, by the way, but more dance-like. I leaf through my collection of psalms in Armenian and wonder which sacred texts accompanied Hrant, since it seems that he'd been able to square his Marxism with a deep religious culture and that his wife, Rakel, was (and probably still is) downright devout. The man who baptized his newspaper *The Furrow* probably had the Parable of the Sower in mind. The seeds that fall from Jesus's hand onto the side of the road, or onto the rocks, are lost, but those that fall on good soil may still bear fruit: one hundredfold, sixtyfold, thirtyfold. This was exactly what *Agos* was—a place where something, rather than nothing, could grow. When Hrant was bombarded with death threats, messages of solidarity from strangers also reached him: "Now that Ramadan has arrived, I pray five times a day, without exception. You are present, my son, in every one of these prayers. I never cease to implore Allah the Most High to protect you." "And me?" asked Hrant in the weekly confession his column had become, "what must I do? Should I strengthen my left-wing conscience by keeping my distance from God or, to the contrary, should I obey my common sense by reciting the psalms of my childhood?" He had learned his prayers by heart at the orphanage, in Turkish and in Armenian, and now, at more than fifty years old, he could still recite several of them. Whereas I only know the beginning of one: "If I forget you, may my right hand forget its skill. May my tongue cling to the roof of my mouth if I do not remember you." Erdem shrugs his shoulders and cites the ever-iconoclastic Jean Kéhayan: "Memory only serves to give one a clear conscience." Not true, I think to myself, that's not true at all.

Awake or asleep I dream, I dream that I'm disintegrating that I'm losing teeth that a white substance is growing inside me, suffocating me, that I bleed out through the hands that my very long nails fall off with a dry snap and blood flows from my skinned legs and slashed throat, I dream of cats falling from balconies, I dream of teenagers with shining eyes who appear from just around the corner and shoot me right in the face, I dream of landslides that sweep Cihangir into the Bosphorus, I dream of ballerinas balancing on tightropes with severed toes, I dream that I'm walking on rooftops overlooking Istanbul and all the tiles begin to come loose. But your hand always catches me, and it's at that same moment that I wake up, head spinning, fists clenched hard into the sheets, even if, as is more and more often the case, you've already left the bed.

Your side of the bed, your bedside table, the ashtray, the sketchbook, taken together they look like ruins. But if I wasn't dreaming, yesterday, when you came home in the middle of the night drunk, and you were seriously drunk, we made love violently, as if I were still capable of fighting, as if there were still some strength left in me to subdue, and I don't even know if you got what you wanted, you fell asleep right away and now it's morning and you're not here.

The window is open and I can hear sounds coming in from the street, it must be late already, I'm covered in sweat, I go straight into the shower and sit there for a long time, a very long time, beneath the scalding water, I shave my legs and tiny cuts leave bloody red dots here and there, and I have impressive bruises on my thighs. When I get out of the shower the room is fogged, I wipe off my smudged makeup and re-apply it—not too bad for someone who's come back from dreams of a thousand deaths. I put on black eyeliner, and as it sometimes happens when I'm really tired—utterly and unfathomably exhausted—my pupils are dilated. My eyes look piercing, my skin is tan. Frankly, I look radiant.

I leave to smoke on the balcony and I spot an untouched cheese pastry on the coffee table. At your desk, your back to me, you stare at the screen, unmoving, perhaps concentrating, perhaps dozing a little, too. I sneak up on you from behind, put my hand on your neck and kiss you from the other side, you don't jump, you stroke my arm distractedly, you say you bought me a pastry but we're out of coffee, I have to go back out. I agree, then you change your mind, you should go have breakfast with Georgi, he's downstairs. I'm going to stay here today, have to work on this. I ask if Georgi is in charge of looking after me now. An annoyed smile. No one's in charge of anyone, you should stand on your own two feet. You end the conversation by getting up, and only now as you grab your cigarettes do you look at me, touch my cheek and smile tenderly this time, asking if I slept well. I say sure, what do you want me to say.

I think he's getting tired of me. Elsa is a good friend and a fabulously expressive conversationalist, she makes a funny face when she says, what else could he want? But also I have to say, you're completely unbearable, little miss twist-the-knife. Sara had warned me of this, that I'd find myself on the other side of a prism that would be my book, that I'd be nothing more than a ghost of my writing, and that life wouldn't be enough for me. But what a joke that is. Doesn't seem to me that he's looking at you like a ghost. She hesitates, pointing her finger at me, but if you dare to write about everything you're telling me here, in your book, you can't be surprised if he starts avoiding you.

Elsa always gives good advice, I think—she's honestly one of the most brilliant people I know, a veritable genius. She landed in Istanbul with only twenty hours of Assimil *Turkish* under her belt, which she completed on the plane, and has managed to win over the whole city. She has a reputation for frequenting bars and concert halls, for drinking like a fish, yet she's somehow always bright and ready for work the next morning. I listen to her dissect my love life as I down beer after beer, after a while I lose track of what she's saying but I know it's perfect, luminous even—it's two in the morning, the bar's closing, and she says, we're only human, after all.

I encourage the small calico cat hanging around the building to come up with me, and it agrees, following me as I climb the stairs, keeping a respectful distance from my staggered ascent. On the third floor, forgetting whether I'm on the third or fourth, I try the lock with my key, but it isn't going to open because I'm not in the right place. Or no, maybe I am, because now the door is open, but it's the neighbour, and he doesn't look very happy to see me. I bow before slipping away and climb one more set of stairs, this time ringing the bell, just to be sure, and yes this is it because he opens the door, his eyes narrowed. I kiss him and say we have to talk. Him: I don't think so, no. He sees the cat behind me, says you've got to be kidding me. He walks the cat back downstairs, I hear the main door open and close, his footsteps coming back up the stairs two at a time. He has my bag in his hand, which apparently I'd forgotten on the third-floor landing, puts it on a chair as I struggle to balance on one foot and take my shoes off with dignity, and he hands me a glass of water. If you want to eat, there are leftovers, I'm going back to bed. I hoist myself onto the kitchen counter and begin to summarize everything Elsa told me, but he doesn't want to hear it. He helps me take off my other shoe and goes to bed. The apartment isn't so big that he can't hear me, not soundproof enough to prevent my babbling from entering his silence, so I continue on my own for a while, though nothing I'm saying makes any sense, neither in English nor French. And then no more. I climb down from my perch, enter the bedroom, turn on the light. He curses Allah, which doesn't happen that often, throws his arm over his face to block out the light. I sit down next to him and touch his chest with my fingertips to see if it's still moving. I tap his tattoos—my favourite, a sheep taking a bite out of a bar code—and I'm elated as if I have good news to announce, I say that Elsa really understood what's wrong with us and that now, thanks to her, I understand, too, I'm so grateful to her, just listen to this: we're only human, after all. He's being nice, at least—he doesn't get angry, just bursts out laughing. No kidding. I'm grateful to you both, indeed. Now he grabs me by the wrist and pulls me into him, and now I can't move and he says, quiet now, and falls asleep. I close my eyes but have to bite my lip to stop myself from saying anything more. I concentrate on counting sheep in Turkish, on matching my breaths, calm and deep, to his.

A text from him: You coming to the Muz? I have an illustrator for you, for Hrant. He's an angel, so nice and funny. I find the Instagram account of the guy, his name is Berkin. Fine, angular, digital strokes; flashy colours, lots of pink and blue, as well as a recurring, likely autofictional character, a smoking dandy wearing big glasses. There are a fair number of sensual drawings of zennes, male belly dancers in drag, typically hired for bachelorette parties. A mural catches my eye, a pile of languid female bodies, a zenne standing in front of it. This could be the moment before the death of Sardanapalus, an androgynous Sardanapalus, wearing a lime-green bra on his waxed chest, a brooding pout, asymmetrical bangs. I wonder what Hrant would have thought of this.

I leave to take the ferry to the European side. Surprisingly, for several weeks now, more and more shoeshiners have planted themselves along the quay, forming a quaint honour guard in front of the fish restaurants in an absurd show of competition. What are the odds that there is sufficient work for eight or ten shoeshiners in a given place? It's as if they've been kicked out of the old town, where they all play the same game to catch tourists: they walk around, lugging their heavy and cumbersome equipment, and when they cross paths with a well-shod foreigner, they "drop" their brush; naturally the victim rushes to retrieve it, and from there unfolds a whole routine from which it's impossible to escape until, shoes shined or not, the vendor has managed to get two or three pounds. Try doing that with locals rushing to catch their ferry in Kadıköy and it's more likely you'll get a brush thrown in your face.

As it happens, I'm wearing flip-flops, so they don't care about me anyway. I grab a sesame seed roll to eat on the boat. The police checkpoint has a squash-all-threats-to-national-security feel. My bag contains the biography of Hrant Dink and a bottle of rakı, which is clearly not enough to assuage the inspector's worries about my possible affiliation with a jihadist organization. She takes her time to look through everything and I stop myself from making a joke. She could make me miss the boat.

Often, between a workday's end and nightfall, musicians accompany the crossing, as well as vendors with their sales pitches for random objects ranging from vegetable peelers to solar garden lamps, all of this going on beneath screens affixed to the ceiling that display endless loops of cooking recipes and cat videos, intended to distract passengers and prevent panic attacks on public transport. This evening there are two singers and a guitarist who apparently prefer to catch the sunset on the deck rather than play inside, even though it's less crowded in here. Even if the light wanted to fall on the city unnoticed, it couldn't—there's something about the skyline, the skyscrapers, the minarets, all working together to make the light bend just so, and then, just as everything is about to fade into oblivion, the city becomes ablaze. Fifteen minutes of magic and then it's like it never happened, it's dark. I get off the boat and head for the funicular, and as I make my way onto a pedestrian street, the heavy bass coming from inside the bars begins to set the tone for the rest of this neighbourhood, which feels increasingly hysterical in relation to the city as the political situation becomes more tense. I put in my earbuds so I don't have to deal with early-evening catcallers or cocaine dealers. In front of the Muz there's some commotion—four boys have started to dismantle the window display. What are you guys doing? They've decided to move the bar to the back, closer to the backyard terrace, and bring the tables for the artists closer to the front, as well as some random, overpriced design stuff they no longer hope to sell, plus a couch for the cats—and for people, too, of course, why not.

On the wall opposite the entrance to the Muz, Georgi and his wife are wielding paintbrushes and writing a new motto, in dancing capital letters, in French: *Le seul moiyen d'affronter un monde sans liberté est de devenir si absolument libre qu'on fasse de sa propre existence un act de révolte. — Albert Camus.* Will you please confirm that this actually means something? I'd never had much confidence in Georgi when he said he spoke French. I tell him we've got plenty of useless letters in French, but he's got a stray *i* in *moyen*. He's unspeakably annoyed.

Berkin is in the middle of a coffee-cigarette break with Zehra, the painter who decorated the bar. Zehra introduces us. Berkin looks just like his drawings, the same way old people look like their dogs. It's funny, you can recognize his silhouette—tall, skinny, slouched—but what you can't see in his drawings is his weathered skin, thin brows, and crow's feet, all of which call attention to the incredible, almost translucent green eyes peeking out from between his long black lashes. Aware of the effect he has on both men and women, he has the warm sociability and easygoing generosity of rich people. Come, let's try out the new couch. Immediately I feel like part of the group. He works for *Ondört Muz*, the newspaper that republished *Charlie*'s cartoons after the attacks and is now being prosecuted for these drawings by the same government that protested with Hollande in Paris back in January. Berkin doesn't care, you know, about the political risks when it comes to freedom of expression—I don't mean to relativize, but there's simply nothing we can do about it. It's pure arbitrariness and completely impossible to predict when, how, or why someone will get angry at a newspaper that has not once been sued or banned, and tear it to shreds anyway. Otherwise, he's freelance, the necessary counterpart to working for the independent press. I have to make a living, I'm basically a whore—it's not entirely unpleasant, by the way. I wonder if I've heard correctly that he just said it's not always bad to play the whore. Right now my main client is in Dubai—everyone with money is in Dubai, right?—that fake country with no culture that thinks itself master of the world. I explain that in French we have an expression to say exactly that, *se prendre pour les rois du pétrole*, to think you're king of the hill. He bursts out laughing, the French are so dumb—I like that, it's funny. So, you have a project about Hrant? He doesn't let me explain a thing, which is just as well. I just want a long-term project with some political and historical significance. Hrant is perfect. Don't bother describing moods or characters to me, just dialogues. What we really need is a point of view. Not only about Hrant, by the way—this is a project that's going to take time, you've really got to get inside it, familiarize yourself with it. But we could try our hand at a short series, we'd publish it one page at a time in the newspaper. Send me some raw dialogue, current events, everyday life, your perspective on Istanbul, anything that makes a scene—and we'll see if I can turn it into drawings. I'm surprised he's so confident, so immediately concrete. Your boyfriend told me you were great, that's enough for me. Here's another thing. He tells me he's in the middle of a divorce, he tried to make a settled life for himself, but at thirty-five he doesn't want to make himself unhappy anymore: he loves men. It doesn't always work out. I mean, I got married when I was young. I wanted children, but the bottom line is I've been miserable ever since and I don't even have kids. What a waste.

Sometimes I ask myself stupid questions, like how do you expect to have a deep relationship—let alone raise children, don't even go there—with a guy who grew up without Jacques Demy's *Donkey Skin,* who doesn't know *Mary Poppins* or *Bluebeard*? Turkish fairy tales all begin with the same phrase: "Once upon a time, or maybe not..." This gives some idea of the broth of precarity in which this country's dreams are steeped. Once upon a time, or maybe not, there were two basket weavers who worked hard, but one had faith and the other didn't. One day, the sultan came to the village and said to them: "I will fill your baskets with wheat. If you take care of them, these seeds will turn into gold coins." This story is recounted by Elif Shafak in her novel *The Bastard of Istanbul,* but she doesn't reveal the outcome. I wonder if the unbeliever threw his grains into a furrow, which would suit me just fine for what I'm cooking up. Instead, Elif Shafak tells stories of pigeons, and also leaves them unfinished. In the novel, the Armenian grandfather, just before being arrested by the police, was putting his finishing touches on a collection of tales he would go on to call *The Little Lost Pigeon and the Peaceful Land.* The hero is a volatile character who flits from city to city collecting stories on the verge of being forgotten. According to Shafak, "at a time when the Ottoman Empire was bubbling with grandiose works, revolutionary movements, and nationalist divisions, and when the Armenian community was thirsty for new ideologies and debates, there was not a single collection of children's stories written in Armenian." The Armenian grandfather's contribution to this collection was to add a story of his own, the tale of the Little Lost Pigeon. "But I warn you," he writes, in the story told by Şafak, "if you say anything sad, I will fly away." And it is here that the storyteller is interrupted by the hatchet of History.

"The bird has flown away. Let's hope the same for the remaining 80 million Turks," chirped the writer Sevan Nişanyan on Twitter. Nişanyan's signature symbol is the snail. He also had a tower built that was dedicated "to the stupidity of the Turkish government," he'd undertaken to reinvest in the old abandoned Greek villages on the coast, close to Ephesus, then was sentenced to sixteen years in prison and bravely served three and a half before setting sail in a daring escape of lightness and irony. An immediate international arrest warrant was issued by the offending government, and political asylum was granted to this former *Agos* columnist by Greece, on the island of Samos, so close to the Turkish coast that when the sky is clear, he can still see the hills of Şirince.

Elsa is talking to me about a book she translated by Pınar Selek, who has been living in exile in France for years, out of the Turkish justice system's reach. It is a story in which Hrant, with his fearful pigeon heart, is the ghostly hero. "It all began with the fall of a young blue pigeon struck by a slingshot. It fell without a sound. [...] A young boy was walking toward the pigeon. We could have sped over and snatched the slingshot, or even taken the bird to safety. We could have tried to save him, all of us together, but we were afraid." Pınar's text is illustrated with engravings by a French artist, Elvire Reboulet. In one of them, we see an old woman with the head of a witch, or a gypsy, or a grandmother, lifting up the wings of the resuscitated pigeon. I learn that this story was adapted for theatre by director and activist Mehmet Atak, under the title *A Fountain of Stories: The Government Doesn't Just Kill by Stealing Lives*. I find his contact information easily and write to him, introduce myself quickly and awkwardly, express my interest in his work. He responds right away, asks me to get a beer with him, asks me how is it possible that we don't already know each other?

Soon after this I dreamed that a bird appeared on a balcony, a kind of stork, and the closer I got to it the smaller it became, and finally I saw a rolled-up message on its foot. It was from you. It said that you were sorry, that you would have liked to say it to me in person, but you couldn't come to my funeral. He was sleeping soundly next to me and I woke him up to tell him the dream, and after a long silence he murmurs, it's not wrong, you know, if you had to be buried in France, with all their visa bullshit, I wouldn't be able to be there. Then an awkward silence.

I write to Berkin to ask if he's good at drawing birds. He sends me a pretty green parrot, like the ones seen in Topkapı Park. I say I want to write a story from the point of view of the pigeons at Taksim Square. I even have a title—not to mention an intense feeling of huge strides being made—*In the Worry of Pigeon Songs*, a subtle reference to Hrant's last article, as well as Bernard-Marie Koltès's play, *In the Solitude of Cotton Fields*. You see? He asks if I've been drinking, in which case it's funny, he wishes me a speedy recovery. By the way, you should know that in Turkish, pretty much the same word is used to refer to *pigeon*, *turtledove*, and *dove*, but Hrant, in his last text, was probably referring to a symbol of peace rather than the crumb collectors of Taksim Square. He encourages me to think a little more about this.

So, you're going to write about Hrant? About Hrant, about Naji, about you. He sighs. Would it be too much to ask to leave me out of it? If you want my opinion—I shake my head no—you don't need this distraction to understand what's happening to us, you could just as easily see it for yourself. Instead of adding all these layers of death for you to hide behind. You won't get anywhere with these millstones around your neck. But that's exactly it, I say, I don't want to go anywhere. I'm staying here.

Did you see the cartoon in *Charlie Hebdo*? As if I could be so cut off from the world that the internet doesn't reach me. It's all I've heard about for the past two days. And? And nothing, I find the cartoon trivial and the reactions insane, as usual. What is this drawing, I don't even understand. Penne? Lasagna? They depicted the victims of the earthquake in Italy crushed into lasagna. Sorry, but I find that completely horrible, extremely offensive. Oh really? Metin scrolls on his phone to find the drawing in question. What's offensive, lasagna? Put yourself in the position of the victims' families, seeing their loved ones caricatured as lasagna. Believe me, they have better things to do than be on Twitter and engage in debate as to whether lasagna is offensive or benign. If journalists didn't rush into the rubble to show them the drawings and get their reaction, they wouldn't think anything of the lasagna. May we ask why you're laughing? If you repeat the word *lasagna* too often in the same sentence it sounds funny, I can't help it, it's just nerves. And if people had laughed after *Charlie*? I shrug, as if some people had actually refrained. You think laughter is a sign of humanity? Some laughter scares me. Bahçeli, get out of that body. Who's Bahçeli? President of the far right: no one, no one on this earth has ever seen him laugh. He must laugh in secret sometimes. What he laughs at is a mystery. Oh wait, I'm sure he laughed the day Hrant was killed—and the staff at *Charlie*, too, I bet they also found it funny.

It's a good question. I ask John, *Charlie*'s archive manager, who sends me the three issues that followed Hrant's assassination. In the first one, dated January 22, 2007, I find an article that gets the date of his death wrong and pokes fun at the conspiracy theories that had begun to flourish across Turkish media, according to which "Turkey's enemies" had created a climate of "provocation" in the country. A few pages later, the political cartoonist Siné's column begins with a selection of press clippings about hunting accidents, which he clearly relishes ("These idiots are doing it on purpose to make me happy, I swear!") and then, without transition, draws a dead bird, almost like a Shadok, legs in the air, three bloody holes in his right side. Siné's loopy letters float around the body. "'My state of mind is as nervous as a pigeon's,' wrote journalist Hrant Dink, of Armenian origin, just one week ago, in the daily newspaper he founded ten years ago in Turkey. He had a keen sense of foreboding: hunters, probably from Turkish nationalist circles, have just shot him three times to teach him not to mention the Armenian genocide ever again."

The following issues do not mention it either, and for good reason. The files that John sends me are labelled "Trial." *Charlie* appeared that week before the 17th Chamber for incitement to racial hatred for republishing the Danish cartoons of Muhammed. In his editorial, Philippe Val renewed his confidence in the institutions of the Republic to protect freedom of expression—while recalling that he had been living for months, like other members of the newspaper, under police protection because of incessant threats. This newspaper I'm flipping through now, fewer than ten years old, is like an open tomb from which familiar voices still escape—just a few pages later, Cavanna writes: "Faced with the audacity of religious interference and the violence of threats, *Charlie Hebdo* unanimously decided to show its solidarity. We were convinced that our colleagues, in France and around the world, were all going to do the same. Need I say that we were rather disappointed? It was a symbolic gesture, of course, as the caricatures were very poor, in inspiration and talent alike, but the threats were not a matter for art criticism. [...] Should we trust the justice system in our country? I'll let you know next week. But come to think of it, you already know the answer!"

I thought the hate campaign against Hrant had begun after *Agos* published an article suggesting that Sabiha Gökçen, one of Atatürk's adopted daughters, Sabiha Gökçen, national icon, Sabiha Gökçen, the first female air pilot, Sabiha Gökçen, the protegée of the first president of the Republic, was a survivor of the Armenian genocide. One of those referred to as "the remnants of the sword." When I explain this to Elsa, she throws her hands up in the air, but seriously, why would anyone publish that? Hrant, summoned and severely warned after publishing such "provocations," justified himself to the Istanbul prosecutor by saying that he didn't want to address the Armenian question in Turkey solely by talking about the dead, that he also wanted to know what had become of the survivors and, more specifically, more intimately, the orphans. From its earliest years, *Agos* had been a repository for testimonies from descendants of Armenians searching for their family members, whom they'd lost track of decades ago. This is how, upon the death of her grandmother, having learned that, contrary to what she'd always believed, she'd inherited a decimated family tree, lawyer Fethiye Çetin published an obituary in *Agos* briefly recounting what she knew of her history, with hopes of finding her exiled parents. It didn't take long for this message in a bottle to make its way across the ocean, and for Hrant, consequently, to contact Fethiye: "Can you come by the newspaper? Your family in America called."

This would become the premise of *My Grandmother*, a bestseller and, for the generation of the 2000s, a major wake-up call regarding the previously concealed journeys of the remnants of the sword. It paved the way for other stories, like that of Jean Kéhayan's family, recounted some years later in *Stateless*—about his newborn mother left for dead in the Syrian desert, buried near an oasis where a jeep of missionaries would find her just in time, "the baby Guldéné resurrected and adopted by a Kurdish family, before joining a Quaker-run orphanage in Aleppo." Or Iştar's nanny. Here's a story for you, Iştar tells me in the middle of dinner, pointing her finger at me like a summons: her name was Mariam (like my mother, I say, this is a good start, but then the entire table turns to me to ask if I'm Armenian, too, as if half the women in the Mediterranean weren't named some variation of Mariam), anyway she lost her daughter during the marches across Anatolia in 1915. Thanks to her, Iştar says, unlike other children of my generation, by the age of ten I knew everything about the Armenian massacres, and believe me, in the 1950s, in Ankara, there weren't very many of us, even among educated Turks, who knew anything about this history. Mariam died in the late 1970s. A few years later, my parents had a visit from the police. We had received a letter from Armenia; at that time, no communication with Armenia was possible, the police had translated the letter before bringing it to us. It was Mariam's daughter who had finally—though too late—found her mother's whereabouts. I'm telling you this so you understand: Hrant opened Pandora's box. He wasn't like the other Armenians, who had lived all those years without daring to speak out. He no longer wanted to be one of those people who hid like insects, who didn't want to know.

Hrant liked to recall the story of Abdullah the Lizard, who stayed in his village despite the deportations, blending in with the local population until the day someone saw him peeing against a wall and started spreading the rumour that he wasn't circumcised. A mob came after him, tracking him back to his house. He hid. They surrounded him, shouting that he wasn't one of us, that he wasn't one of them—I don't know how to say it. Eventually a neighbour intervenes, tries to calm things down, then enters the house to take the scapegoat's hand. What he gets in return is a bloody piece of skin. He leaves and asks the mob that Abdullah the Lizard, newly circumcised out of fear, be left alone. Perhaps then, at last, the group understands that it has gone too far. Another fable haunts Hrant's memory, a story told by his brother, who got it from who knows where. During this same time of manhunts, an Armenian farmer is preparing to abandon his farm, as he has been ordered to leave. It will be spring soon, and his threshing machine is broken, and he's determined to repair it before he leaves. A neighbour asks him why he is being so stubborn, since he's probably leaving for good. The Armenian responds that he has sown the seeds, and someone will come to harvest them. Do you want the person in charge of threshing the wheat to find a machine that doesn't work? In a posthumously published text, Hrant asks us, "Where is the threshing machine? Let's find it and repair it, for a start."

When I ask Yetvart Danzikian, the current director of *Agos*, about this, he smiles at how far we've come since the Sabiha Gökçen scandal of 2004. Back then, Atatürk and his army were a force to be reckoned with! Today, you see what the government does with these symbols of the Republic. In fact, President Erdoğan himself officially apologized for the Dersim massacres in which Sabiha Gökçen participated, when he found it useful to kill two birds with one stone: a gesture toward the Kurds and a shot in the foot for Atatürk's heirs. I'm sure that today we could say pretty much anything about Sabiha—that she was Armenian, Greek, even Jewish! It would go off without a hitch. I ask if, to Turkish nationalists, being Jewish is worse than being Armenian. Yetvart wavers, goes back and forth a bit, but no. Armenian remains the ultimate insult.

But I'm way off the mark. I mean sure, the Sabiha affair was a turning point, but what really sparked the controversy was a different article published in *Agos*, a series of six texts written by Hrant on Armenian identity, one of which, when taken out of context and exploited, made its author public enemy number one. Hrant pointed out that the evil figure of the Turk, particularly in the imagination of the diaspora, was the pillar of Armenian identity—and that it was urgent to get rid of this poison and let the young independent Armenia irrigate, with new blood, the common ground of community scattered throughout the world. Then I reread that sentence because the allegory is pretty convoluted—it's a rephrasing of a sentence by Atatürk about the glorious blood of the Turkish race, and I'm not sure I fully get it, but clearly one would have to read it in extremely bad faith to understand it as a call to spread the impure blood of the Turks by force. Except that there was no shortage of bad faith—because despite Hrant's explanations, the unambiguous context of the newspaper dedicated to the peaceful coexistence of communities, and the textual analyses commissioned from various specialists, nothing was enough, and the accusation of racism persisted. In 2010, three years after Hrant's death, the Turkish government, questioned by the European Court of Human Rights, had not changed its interpretation one bit. Renowned linguist Necmiye Alpay noted this in an article in which she attempted to restore some truth: "The defence of the murderer and that of the Turkish government is based on the same accusation! [...] The reader's duty is to be honest with the text and its author." But she also noted, not without weariness, that "writings containing irony, metaphors, and colourful expressions are less likely to be understood. Especially when one has prejudices or lacks common sense."

Hrant had no idea that his article would have such grave consequences. He even congratulated himself for having succeeded at clashing with both Armenian nationalists and Turkish nationalists. It was a journalist who threw the first stone, turning Hrant's words against him, outraged at his use of the expression "Turkish poison" in Armenian blood that needed to be purified, and in its wake political leaders rushed to add their fuel to the fire. Protests began in front of *Agos*, first once, then twice, led by an ultra-nationalist who wouldn't let up on Hrant until he was dead. They laid a funeral wreath in front of the newspaper, close to where Hrant was murdered. And the police did nothing, and the press did not report it—except for *Özgür Gündem*, the pro-Kurdish newspaper that would not wait until 2016 to stand in the way of the government's dictatorship—as well as a few isolated examples, such as Aslı Erdoğan, the name everyone now knows, who can be seen in a photo from 2006 at the *Agos* offices alongside Hrant, at a time when the threats were really intense. Behind the camera was Erdal Doğan, the lawyer who defended Hrant and who now, more than ten years later, would defend Aslı. No matter where or how I pick up this story, I always come back to the same people—so few of them that the absence of one must make their world feel orphaned, depopulated. Aslı wrote, before the immense wave of solidarity that Hrant's death would unleash in Turkey: "Were there really so many of us? Then why did we feel so alone for so many years? Why had we spent so much time in this seclusion that had been imposed upon us? I would so much have wanted for what brought us together not to have been a murder. I would have wanted for us, in returning to life, to our respective lives, not to find so many defeats, disappointments, disillusions." This article, published by the Turkish press, was sent to various European newspapers, none of whom took up the offer to republish. Only one Belgian newspaper reprinted it, in an abridged version. It took ten years for the machine to close in on Aslı, for the movement of solidarity she'd hoped for to finally emerge abroad, accompanying her during her four months of detention in 2016, with Necmiye Alpay, at the Bakırköy women's prison.

Bakırköy is a suburb of Istanbul, home to many recent immigrants to the city. It is welcoming, off the beaten path, inexpensive, and home to, among other things, a psychiatric hospital, a courthouse, a prison, and a Turkish–Armenian publishing house founded in 1996 by Hrant and his brothers, paired with a bookstore dedicated to Turkey's minorities called Beyaz Adam, "The White Man." Hrant had no experience in publishing, nor in bookselling—but he already had a jewellery store named after his wife, Rakel, and a handful of other eclectic businesses that would make you smile if they didn't serve as reminders that this man who had come from nothing could have become anything other than one of the most emblematic and therefore vulnerable spokespeople for the Armenian cause. On board the ferry across the Sea of Marmara, the crowd is mixed: people going to Atatürk Airport, workers making the long crossing on the often rough sea on this side. We sail along the sublime shore of the old city, Hagia Sophia and the Blue Mosque facing each other, snubbing us; and Yenikapı, the old "new gate" to Constantinople, is today largely overtaken by the sprawling development of the metropolitan area; our small boat passes easily between the immense cargo ships moored at the mouth of the Bosphorus. At the end of the Bakırköy quay is a trendy fish restaurant and a marina. A Kurdish bakery, men playing backgammon on a terrace, commercial streets. It feels like I'm somewhere else, in Eastern Europe perhaps, or a seaside town. I wander through the streets of the city centre, everything seems boring, ugly, and provincial, including this shop crammed with lurid plastic merchandise framed by two giant posters promoting Elif Shafak's latest book. Is this actually a bookstore? The logo depicts, curiously enough, a donkey reading, seen from behind, showing its ass ostentatiously. No way this is Hrant Dink's bookstore. But then I go inside and immediately recognize the place—I saw a photo of it in the biography, Hrant sitting on a high stool like the ones on which the booksellers are sitting now, glued to their phones. In my photo, he has his arms crossed, clearly talking to someone off-camera, the shelves behind him packed with haphazardly arranged books. Today it's tidier. There aren't many people in the literary fiction section—current bestsellers, a few translations of Georges Bataille and Bernard Lewis. In the "ethnic publications" section, a sampling of books by and about Hrant, but only some of them. A few in Armenian, none in English. I leave to eat a kebab in a cheap café where moustached men are eating lunch without looking at their plates, their noses raised toward a television playing music videos. Then I take the ferry in the other direction with the travellers in transit between Atatürk Airport—scheduled to close soon and be replaced by a new one, Sultan Erdoğan's big project, the largest airport in the world and one that will, it is understood, definitively bury Atatürk—and the equally saturated airport on the Asian shore. Close to Tuzla, where Hrant and Rakel spent the best years of their life together, Istanbul's "low-cost" airport bears the name of the orphan girl who brought about the Dink scandal: Sabiha Gökçen.

A photo taken in Tuzla in the eighties: Hrant and Rakel pose with a dozen young girls next to a lily pond, a lush garden filled with exotic plants, the white and red bricks of the building peeking through from behind them. These same bricks, which haven't moved but have changed colour, may be seen in a photo taken in the same place in 2015, during a concert in support of the summer camp threatened with permanent destruction and for which loads of activists mobilized, the same ones who came out for Gezi, clinging to the urban remnants of Istanbul's multiculturalism. I recognize the musicians: it's the same blues trio with the glowing singer and blurry accordionist. I'm not surprised to see them there. On a wall of the camp, there's some graffiti depicting a three-quarter view of Hrant's face, the same photo that's on the cover of Tuba Çandar's book, used as a stencil, against a backdrop of mountains, birds, and a sign that reads: *Kamp Armen*. Below it is a quotation from one of Hrant's texts: "It is not in my nature to abandon the flames of hell to join the sweetness of paradise. I'm just a man who has set for himself the goal of transforming the hell we live in into paradise."

In Tuzla, in the sixties and seventies, Hrant, his brothers, and their friends built this summer camp themselves—they joke that the orphanage kids' summer camp wasn't exactly ready-made. They spent months making cement, building walls, landscaping the garden, and looking across the fence at another school that had the means to be a real vacation spot for the children, but despite this (or indeed because of it), it became their Atlantis. To top it all off, legend has it that it was in Tuzla that fifteen-year-old Hrant fell in love with Rakel. It was also in Tuzla that they were married, in Tuzla that they had their children. In the meantime, the camp director had been thrown in prison, so Hrant and Rakel took over. Then it was Hrant's turn to spend some time in Turkish prisons, along with his brother, accused after the 1980 coup of being close to radical Armenian Marxist movements. Locked up for weeks in bathrooms converted into cells less than a square metre in size, they were beaten and forced to sing the national anthem, day and night, without stopping. Hrant would go on to write, "It's hard to believe that these men thought they were teaching us love for our country. Not then, not today, not ever, are we the kind of people who can be forced to learn the national anthem in a toilet."

Hakan Günday recently wrote a terrifying novel that features a wicked jailer who keeps dozens of undocumented migrants in an underground "depot" where they wait, at his mercy, for benevolent smugglers to cross the Mediterranean (and that's if they're lucky). This trauma is collective. Hakan Günday's protagonist sings the national anthem to his desperate prisoners while they're killing each other and wallowing in their own shit. Günday writes: "And the nation ends just like it began: to the sound of 'The March of Independence,'" which Turkish children still sing in a line in the schoolyard every Monday and Friday.

Fear not, the crimson flag, waving in these dawns will never fade,
Before the last hearth that is burning in my nation vanishes.
That is my nation's star, it will shine;
That is mine, it belongs solely to my nation.

Oh coy crescent, do not frown for I am ready to sacrifice myself for you!
Please smile upon my heroic nation, why that anger, why that rage?
If you frown, our blood shed for you will not be worthy.
Freedom is the right of my nation who worships God and seeks what is right.

I have been free since eternity, and free shall I be.
What fool dares to shackle me? I defy the temerity!
I am like a roaring flood; I overflow trampling down my banks,
I tear apart mountains, surge into depths, and surpass.

Western horizons may be encircled by walls armoured in steel
But I have my chest brimful of faith as my homeland's frontier.
Let it howl, fear not! How can it smother such solid faith
That single-fanged monster, "Civilization!" as you call it?

My friend! Never ever let the dastards into my land!
Render your body a shield; bring this heinous raid to an end.
For soon shall break the blissful days God promised, for sure;
Perhaps tomorrow, who knows, perhaps even sooner than that.

Do not assume what you tread on is mere "earth", recognize it!
Think of the thousands, without shrouds, lying beneath.
You're the son of a martyr, take shame, hurt not your ancestor;
Cede not this heavenly homeland, even if it's the worlds
you're granted.

Who would not offer his life for this homeland of paradise?
Martyrs would pour forth, all martyrs,
should one simply clutch the earth!
If God will, He may take my life, my beloved, and my wealth,
But may He not, for the world, just deprive me of my homeland.

The sole wish of my soul, oh glorious God, from You is that,
No heathen would ever, on the bosom of my temple, lay hand!
These calls to prayer, whose testimonies are the ground of religion,
Should resound far and wide over my eternal homeland.

Then, my tombstone, if any, prostrates in rapture a thousand-fold,
Of my every wound, oh glorious God, tears of blood gush forth,
And out spurts my corpse, in pure spirit, from the ground,
Perhaps then, shall ascend and to the heavens touch my crown!

So ripple and wave, like dawning skies, oh glorious crescent,
So that every drop of my blood finally be blessed and worthy!
Neither you nor my race shall ever be annihilated,
For my flag, who has lived ever freely, has the right to liberty;
For my nation, who worships God, has the right to independence!

Hrant, according to translator Dominique Eddé, addressed his reader not as one person in need of persuading, but rather as two people in conflict whom he hoped to bring closer together. Karin Karakaşlı, his long-time partner at *Agos*, says he "invented a language that wholly seizes nationalism by the throat." I flip through all the translations I can find, in English and in French, while sitting outside my favourite cafés, where I seem to attract frequent demonstrations of sympathy from neighbours and servers. Erol, the souvenir seller just next to the Muz, is the only one who doesn't hide his disappointment. If you write about Hrant, there won't be any room in your book for me, even though you promised. I ask if he has any stories about Hrant but he shrugs, I'm just a humble shopkeeper. I point out that Hrant himself had a slew of businesses before going into journalism, but Erol doesn't want to be a character in a book about Hrant. I remember the day I saw on TV that he'd died, I didn't know who he was, but I heard it was an Armenian journalist killed by a Turk and trust me: it was the first time in my life I'd ever felt so Turkish, so ashamed of being Turkish. I'd be happy to play the villain, but in a fiction. Whatever your thing is, it hits too close to home. Erol's souvenir shop is trying to change with the times, as Westerners are scarce and have been somewhat replaced by tourists from the Gulf region who, in addition to buying traditional soaps, napkins, magnets, and tchotchkes, acquire calligraphies that

Erol can't read but that he sells as authentically Turkish. I'd sell anything, he says, as long as I can take some time off and ride around with my friends. I ask who he votes for, but he dodges the question—I don't do politics, I'm for peace, I just want everyone to respect each other, that's it. He still does *some* politics, though—I mention the Syrian guy he'd hired but eventually asked to leave. He wanted to do his prayers and he entirely has that right, Erol contends, but he couldn't just abandon the store like that without letting me know. And then he bothered the customers at the Muz because the music was too loud, it was all too much. It's a shame, because it was nice having someone who could speak Arabic to customers, but there's always trouble with Middle Easterners. I burst out laughing, hearing him say this, but he doesn't know what he's said that's funny—just so you know, it's Europe here. "The difference between East and West," writes Hakan Günday, "is Turkey. I don't know if Turkey is the result of subtraction, but I do know that the distance that separates East and West is as wide as the country itself." And within this space emerges a third path, which occurs in any space between two things—without which Europe wouldn't be Europe and the Middle East would be seen as a flat, illegible mess. Erol tried to hire Fares, who's tired of making coffee at the Muz, but Fares declined without a second thought—the ridiculously low wages, twelve hours a day, six days per week, plus his total indifference toward the work. And why not shine the shoes of Emiratis, too, while we're at it. Erol gets it but can only bemoan his own situation, because of course he too would prefer to have a garage filled with old motorcycles. And to live closer to İzmir, spend the day doing nothing—like you, by the way, living *la dolce vita*. I wonder what it is you see in this place. If I weren't stuck here, I'd be long gone. If I had a foreign girlfriend, easy, I'd marry her, and we'd go to Europe. You see, the problem with having me in your book is that I have no intention of dying for this country.

Erol's wife comes into the back where we're chatting quietly, scowls at me, and in an ostensibly polite gesture she takes away our cups of tea, as if to get me to leave, all the while proposing that I have another. But because I insist on leaving now, despite the rain, she gives me a henna, pressing the ball of paste into the palm of my hand, and tells me to dig my nails in and hold on tight, for as long as possible. Afterwards, one can tell by the colour of your hands if you're a loyal woman. I walk out into the rain, henna in hand, it's already dark, I pass by the Muz again and the street seeps, wet and ominous. I'm soaked, the Muz is locked, but I see there's still some light upstairs, and I've no desire to walk all the way to the bus stop that would take me back to the Asian side. I holler up, wiping off my makeup that must be a mess by now anyway. The voice that answers sounds off, he says he'll explain but that right now he can't come down, he's going to throw down the keys from the window. He mumbles, his voice dark, though I assume I've misheard, hopefully I won't hurl myself down along with the keys. The window opens, the keys fall, and miraculously they don't fall onto the awning. I collect them from the gutter, take the stairs normally reserved for employees, and from the back of the room I'm welcomed by a groan and the sound of a slumping body. I take off my shoes, drenched, grimacing as I pass the mirror. He's sitting on the edge of the couch, pale, looking at his shoes. What is happening. I don't know, he says, I felt like clearing my head, I took some stuff. I'm really not okay. I touch my hand to his clammy forehead.

What can I do, I pour a glass of water and get some aspirin, but in the time it takes for me to get rid of that stupid ball of henna—which has now turned my fingers scarlet red—he has lain down. I crouch next to him, holding the water, and wonder if I should call the doctor—but what doctor, with the few Turkish words I know, without knowing what he took. What are you looking at, he grumbles. He says his mind is racing, he can't make it stop. This must be it, when people claim to see their whole life flash before their eyes: I'm going to die. At least I won't have to leave the country... He wavers, gives up on finishing the sentence. What a shame to die now, my brother was going to visit tomorrow morning. He mumbles again that he's sorry I have to see him like this, but it's still better than having left me in the rain, no? I agree, and he looks reassured. He seems so stressed by the idea of dying before I'd gotten shelter that I feel compelled to tell him that even if he *had* died, I wouldn't have blamed him for the rain. He sighs as if I'd just given him the last rites. What a drama queen, I say, caressing his forehead as one would a child's. Come to bed, I'm cold. I snuggle up next to him, he stumbles through an incomprehensible muddle of Turkish and English, then quiets. After several minutes of total silence, I put my hand on his chest, and he jumps as if I were about to strangle him. What now? I just wanted to make sure you were still breathing. That doesn't even matter, he hisses, returning at once to his coma. He doesn't let go of my hand, minutes pass—then he regains consciousness, climbs strenuously up my forearm as if mounting a steep hill, finally arriving at my sleeve: take off your clothes. Now this is funny, I'd really like to see him try to have sex in this state, so I go with it. Outright hallucinating, he says he's seeing double and this brings him back to life, *what luck*, a threesome I can't refuse. As loquacious as he is unintelligible. He rises, but just as soon as his feet touch the floor he collapses. He dissolves into laughter, I can't stand up, incredible, he asks me to get his cigarettes, and I tell him you can't be serious, you aren't going to smoke on top of all this. Of course I am. He hoists himself up and sits on the edge of the mattress as if it's a cliff, gingerly lighting his cigarette and asking me to keep a respectful distance so as not to get burned. He is extremely careful not to burn the bed, nor the rest of the furniture, careful, careful. I love these exaggerated gestures, and he laughs without seeming to know what's funny, stop laughing at me, I'm dying. Behind his eyes is a joy I haven't seen in a long time, and he grabs me by the feet, kisses my knees, my hips, my sex, come here—I want to make love.

When I wake up the next day it's already noon, and I'm alone. If it weren't for the glass of water and aspirin still on the coffee table, I would think I was the one who'd hallucinated. But on my skin lingers the distinct vibration of last night's embrace. I tell myself that if for whatever reason I got pregnant from last night, I would keep it—at this point it wouldn't make much of a difference. That child would look like us: a brat sprung from the edges of consciousness.

I go downstairs, the four of them are sitting around the bar, and they welcome me with smiling, cheerful faces that are at once a little mocking, a little friendly. I tell him he looks better than he did last night, and he tries to look serious, but I can tell he's still a little high. I'm curious, I venture, do you even remember what happened last night? He looks up at the sky, thank God, yes. Puffs out his chest and preens like a child—I was really good, wasn't I?

Ramadan has hardly started, but it's clear that this year will be a tough one. June is the worst time of year to fast, the days are long, the heat is unbearable—this is going to be tense. A mob of fanatics pounces on an event hosted by a small record store in Cihangir, where they make a scene as if to set an example, vandalizing the store and beating up customers who were drinking beer and listening to the new Radiohead album. The incident goes viral on social media and ignites an outrage that's hard to pinpoint. It's the boys from Tophane who are behind it, sighs Ahmet, who lives right at the border of the hipster district of Cihangir and the Tophane area, which is overshadowed by the mosque. At night we see them roam around in small groups, they communicate among themselves and intervene as soon as something upsets them. And no one does anything about it. A retired guitarist, now a programmer for one of Istanbul's most beautiful concert halls that hosts rock, jazz, and indie artists from all over the world, Ahmet is what Georgi calls a Kemal type, joking about their forthcoming extinction, the sons of the secular Turkish middle class; brought up on European culture, they are increasingly in the minority, unprepared to live in a country whose power dynamics they never could have anticipated would undergo such total reversal. Just down the road from Orhan Pamuk's Museum of Innocence, Ahmet's apartment is a haven for all the artists of Cihangir when it comes time to drink beer and listen to music. A vinyl collector, he scours the neighbourhood second-hand record stores, all of them know him from a mile away. I ask if he's heard from the guy down below who'd been beaten by the mob from the mosque. He says it was a new guy, not from around here, a Korean immigrant. It was almost as if to apologize on behalf of his country that Ahmet called the owner of the record store who, though rattled, declared that he would reopen his doors as soon as possible. Radiohead posted a sympathetic statement on Facebook, which boosted the owner's spirits, but Ahmet wasn't impressed. If they had the courage to come play at the protest tonight, I would have thought that was great. But "peace and love" platitudes posted on Facebook from London just aren't enough. A support rally has been announced to take place this evening in front of the record shop. The police are urging everyone to stay home. Ahmet doesn't know if there's really a chance it'll get violent, but because it's just below his place he'll show up, and I might as well stop by, too. By the way, he just bought a Bash Hong record, a real marvel—I make him repeat the name over and over again, desperate to understand what he's talking about—do I know it, I must not be familiar with it, *what* are you saying? No, you *must* know it, and on and on, and we play this guessing game for several minutes before I land on Alain Bashung, *yes*, of course—now get over here, you can translate it for me.

The neighbourhood is already surrounded by the police. The corner store is closed up, we can't buy any beer, which Ahmet says is no big deal, we'll get some delivered. I ask if the delivery guys work during Ramadan, and he raises his eyebrows, are you serious, do you think you're in Saudi Arabia or what. What's the point of having beer delivery if they don't work during Ramadan. On the coffee table, Bashung floats in the dark waters of *Fantaisie militaire*.

Ahmet's ear is turned toward France these days, he's even bringing a few French bands to the street music festival that's coming up. You saw the cops in the street. We're going to get tear-gassed; it'll remind us of Gezi. Wait, before we go down, can you translate this for me? He plays "La nuit je mens." *Je m'en lave mes mains dans le Vercors à l'élastique:* untranslatable. Sorry. Disappointed, he listens in silence, cigarette dangling from his lips, looking out the window at what's brewing down below. Lyrics that speak to me alone and that seem to have something to tell me, assuming the shape of a bubble, a ghost that only I can perceive and that follows me when, with some nervousness, we leave the apartment to join the crowd in front of the record store. It doesn't last long. Barely begun, the protest is violently broken up by the police, and we cough our way back to the apartment, eyes red, we shut the windows tight so we can breathe inside, but after an hour of stewing in our anger, our powerlessness, it's ultimately the heat that stifles us. We decide to go dancing and migrate to Taksim Square; on the way, we run into the infamous militia from Tophane, they watch us pass, sure of themselves, playing the bullies, casting contemptuous glances. Some insults are exchanged. Ahmet immediately calms the situation, as he's known in the neighbourhood and has already had his share of threats that have struck as close as his street, under the pretext that he played music too late, too loud. We shouldn't aggravate them, it wouldn't take much for things to get ugly. He seems wound up afterwards, snarling that people ought to organize counter-militias, that they would need to be armed, too, and ready to move, to show once and for all who sets the rules at night in Istanbul, because we can't count on the police.

It's only when we get to the rooftop that Ahmet calms down. Beer helps more than my jokes, which inevitably fall flat—Elif Shafak is right to point out that it's thanks to her fondness for alcohol that Turkey occasionally resembles a democracy. Luckily Ahmet is already drunk when, in the middle of the night, he receives a cancellation message from one of the groups that was scheduled to come to the street music festival. They'd heard about the scene at the record shop, as well as the police violence this evening. The message, written in French and roughly translated into English, is appalling. That, seen from Paris, Istanbul doesn't seem like a place where musicians really thrive, everyone understands that. But how could anyone be so cruel as to tell Turkish people, who are caught between fundamentalism and authoritarianism, that, well, *we* like to drink and make music, not risk our lives for pleasure. Ahmet hides his disappointment behind nervous laughs, attributing to mere ignorance the snide tone of the email. I'm livid. He raises his glass: long live arrogance, long live France.

The city moves in slow motion. Some shopkeepers are closing early so they can go to dinner. Certain cafés have temporarily stopped serving alcohol. I wonder if I'll have to part ways with my little reading spot on the benches facing the sunset in Üsküdar, but I note that the tea vendors in this conservative neighbourhood are still keeping busy despite their fasting. I linger here one evening with Hrant Dink under my arm, and when the time comes to have a drink, the motorcycle comes by to pick me up. I love riding into the Muz's courtyard, as if passing through the Blue Mosque's monumental doorway as the sultans once did, staying up on their horses, just to make a spectacle of it. Childish pride. I take off my helmet. In lieu of driver's licences, we have invested in brand-new helmets, betting on the fact that cops would never stop motorcyclists who have two helmets *and* wear them (the general practice is to ride with no helmet, or with a helmet attached to the handlebars). I wave to those I see sitting outside: Berkin, and the small group of cartoonists for *Ondört Muz* who are pretending to work in the sun. Anna is alone inside, behind the bar. She barely acknowledges my hello, grabs a glass, and as she pours from the percolator I see her hand trembling, strange, I've never seen her like this before, she really is shaking, she lowers the full cup onto its saucer and seems hardly in control of her hands as she does this, the coffee nearly spilling all over the bar. I ask again if she's okay. She cleans the side of the coffee machine with extreme concentration. It's as if she hasn't heard me. Anna, are you all right? There was a weird guy who came by just now. She doesn't want to say more, she makes a gesture that indicates that we're no longer alone. But I carry on anyway, waving over the others, what do you mean a weird guy, she puts a finger to her mouth to say no but then she surrenders, at least wait for them all to be here so I don't have to repeat myself. A guy came in this afternoon when there was no one here, he came to the bar and grabbed me, he dragged me to the storage room and took me by the throat and I wanted to fight back but he hit me against the wall and then I remembered I should yell so I screamed and then he left, he just left. I want to say something comforting, but he cuts me off, what do you mean that happened here this afternoon, with the guys outside? No, they hadn't arrived yet, there was no one here. He raises his voice, but why didn't you call us, she shakes her head no, he slams his helmet on the bar, where is he, what does he look like, she starts to explain but he cuts her off, increasingly furious, did he speak Turkish? What was he wearing? Would you recognize him? She says yes, of course, he's been here before, but why didn't you kick him out right away and call the neighbours for help—I see her begin to cower and it breaks my heart, now it's my turn to yell, fuck it's not her fault, he shoots me a glare and leaves to take his anger out on the group of artists sipping their beers outside. Now it's all hands on deck, they're all riled up, going up and down the block, scanning the passersby, Anna stands in the doorway, trembling, arms crossed over her long yellow dress. As if he would come back right after, I say, and then what, they're going to kill him? She shrugs, and why not, men could stand to die a little, too. I ask if she wants to go home, if she wants us to go somewhere else, but she refuses, absolutely not, I want to stay here, I work until ten. She's stubborn, no way she'd leave her post, and, in any case, she doesn't want to go home, she asks us not to tell Fares, who will just get upset if he finds out about this, he'd already made a comment this morning about her dress. I'm horrified. But she says she'd like some vodka if I can find some. I accept the mission. Passing in front of his store, I alert Erol, who seems at once sorry and not surprised, he says, not the least bit maliciously, girls, what can you do, you know it happens, we have to live with it. I want to smash the bottle over his head. I go back to the Muz, the cartoonists have returned to their table, resumed their conversation and now have the nerve to ask for a drink. Berkin is at the bar alone and asks if we can watch the security camera videos, see if his face was caught, but of course the cameras aren't set up properly, the images are useless. I say we have to report it anyway, but he winces, you know that cops here just make things worse. I insist they do something, but what, in any case Anna doesn't have valid papers, so forget the police, it'll only cause problems for all of us. I think about this, Anna stays quiet, Berkin seems distraught; Erol closes his shop and comes over, no doubt to show his support, but when he hugs her all he can say is that her bright yellow dress during Ramadan maybe wasn't the best idea. And now I'm really fed up, listening to them explain that it's too much to expect anything better, there are assholes everywhere and you have to be realistic and protect yourself—a rift erupts among us. Stop making this face like we're defending the guy, we're just trying to say that these apes are at home here, and none of your feminist theories can do anything about it. The least bit of skin is provocation enough for them, simple as that. Do you think we enjoy this? Welcome to Turkey. Their voices get louder and Anna, panicked, apologizes, and I'm furious at the guys for taking her apology as proof that they're right. Berkin must think that speaking to me as if I were a toddler will calm me down, the other just pretends not to hear, but I can tell he's annoyed, on edge, and Berkin ultimately asks me to go back to the apartment instead of getting everyone all worked up. No way. But he insists he doesn't want me here in this state. What state, because I'm angry, because I'm upset, don't we have the right to be? I repeat that we should go to the cops and that if none of them have the balls to do it I'll go with Anna myself, but he says in Turkish—and for the first time ever the language is unambiguous, clear, I understand each and every word—if she says one more time that we need to go to the police I'm going to lose it. He starts to raise his arm but stops midway, a gesture I interpret wrongly, perhaps, as if he were going to hit me, I throw his helmet and the pile of newspapers on the ground and suddenly he yells, get the hell out of here, you don't understand anything, and you aren't helping anyone.

I've been alone in the apartment for one week. No news. He came by only to grab some of his stuff, found a bag and stuffed it with clothes without a word, while I stayed in the living room, trying to find something to say. On his way out, one hand already on the door, he said there you go, it's all yours. You can stay as long as you want, write about me, or others, I don't give a shit, you're on your own. I'm too busy trying to save myself and the Muz, I can't handle you on top of all this, then he left. I make considerable effort not to move his things. The tobacco tin remains open next to the computer, the newly washed glass turned upside down next to the sink. I wait two days to wash the dishes.

I talked to Yemliha about it, and she decided to count to three. If he hasn't come back by Friday, I'll fly in to spend the weekend with you. I'd been bragging about this apartment for a long time anyway. On Friday—still no word from him—she buys a ticket, packs a bag, jumps on the plane, and in the early evening she arrives at Sabiha Gökçen Airport. We meet in the empty terminal. She is sprightly and cheerful, excited to have arrived so quickly, so easily, and she's ready to celebrate. We take the bus that goes through some neighbourhoods undergoing construction, riding past towers, mosques, shopping malls, and then cross the bridge, arriving on the European side of the Bosphorus, where we meet some friends to have drinks at a bar with a view. What a thrill. We order cocktails, make conversation with our neighbours. Elsa is there, and she has nothing more to say about my situation that she didn't already say last time: *We're only human, after all.* She seems to have made a friend, a tall and spectacularly bearded dark-haired man. He reminds me of someone, and I ask him why that could be; he says he's an accordionist in a blues band. The only way to get home after the bar closes is a group taxi that crosses the Bosphorus Bridge from Taksim. We walk along the pedestrian streets, still crowded during these early morning hours, an underworld of drug dealers, folks stumbling home, the pulsing bass rhythms echoing from nearby concert halls. I try to make conversation with the accordion player, and even though he hardly speaks English and my Turkish is entirely lacking, I can't help but laugh at his giant beard, which he strokes as he looks at me with utter seriousness, his Christlike face. Ceremoniously he takes out some beers from his bag and we make a toast, tapping the bottles to the ground, to the absent and the dead. We walk toward the square, the accordion player runs from left to right, playing the clown. Suddenly I spot a familiar face—Metin, who automatically looks around for my usual companion, waves to me with some reluctance, as well as to the accordion player, who in return takes a bow. Glancing toward my sidekicks, he asks if I'm on my way back to Kadıköy, I say yes, and he nods. He notes that I should probably avoid walking around with a bottle in the middle of Ramadan; the mad Christ runs around us, hands flung in the air, and suddenly Metin remembers, he was at Gezi, wasn't he? The accordion player tips an invisible hat. Elsa asks Metin if he wants to have a nightcap, and even though I understand neither where nor how this will happen—it's past four in the morning—it becomes clear that Elsa is going home with him. Yemliha says, okay, let's go, Elsa has obviously found something better to do. Jesus, you coming?

It would appear so. He comes back to the apartment with us. The day rises through the window, the couch is quickly transformed into a bed for the guest, Yem will sleep with me, and we're not too worried about the squatter, who, it appears, has decided to make himself some pasta. We go to bed. After sleeping for a few hours I get up for some water and he's asleep on the floor just outside our room, in the doorway, shirt half-open, one leg leaning against the wall, at least he found a pillow, head tilted, mouth open, like a tossed rag doll. He sleeps soundly, arm outstretched and spoon in hand, a bowl of macaroni on the floor a little farther away, out of reach. I burst out laughing. With my glass of water, I step over him, still giggling, unable to stop, and return to bed.

When we rise, we nearly trample the musician as we make our way out of the room. He is still sleeping, folded into a fetal position at our door; Yem taps his cheek to check for life. We drape a blanket over him and leave to go get some fresh air. We order fresh-pressed orange juice from a sidewalk vendor who chuckles at the sight of our tired faces. Elsa has given us a time to meet her on the quay, I don't know where she's coming from, probably from Metin's as she lives on this side of the Bosphorus, and when I see how terrible Yem and I look, I can hardly imagine Elsa, who likely did more than just sleep at Metin's. But then a taxi pulls up in front of us and stops, the door opens to reveal the blue flowered dress from last night: Elsa is dazzling. It's as if she's just stepped out of a time machine, or maybe it's Yemliha and me who have aged thirty years. The ferry passes us slowly on the quay, we look at one another, and in an instant we make the silent and unanimous decision to run to the pier and board it. We settle in on the roof, and the wind revives us. Seagulls fly overhead, Yemliha dozes, Elsa takes smiling selfies that she sends to Metin. We eat sweet breads and sip tea during the entire ride, weaving along the Golden Horn up until the Eyüp Sultan Mosque, where the ferry lets us off with the pilgrims who have come to gather around the tomb of the Prophet's companion. The tourists walk toward the cemetery in search of Pierre Loti, and then there's the three of us, in the middle of it all, eating ice cream and petting stray cats.

My fingers are still orange with henna, but now my nails are gnawed. I could just send him a message, of course, but then what. What if he doesn't answer, et cetera. I know where to find him, he probably hasn't left the Muz, and the certainty of finding him there when I want is how I've gotten this far, waiting for him to be the one to come back. I don't even know how angry either of us is. But the doubt is becoming unbearable. What if he's really gone. I decide to go and find out.

There are tons of people just outside the Muz, motorcycles, too, and immediately I identify the surrounding shopkeepers, this small neighbourhood team of tattooed arms. He's there, too, in rapt conversation with a cool Kurdish girl with a ridiculous little dog, I think I saw her perform at a concert once, and she seems to recognize me, too, because by the time I reach them, she has slipped away. He welcomes me as if nothing has happened, as if I were just passing by. We are going on a ride to Belgrad Forest, trying to enjoy a bit of the Bosphorus, this beautiful night. I don't care, I point toward the street corner—and her? He turns back, and with the BMW also parked on the corner he pretends to not understand, what, the motorcycle? I insist, though I know I shouldn't. He looks me straight in the eyes and asks, what do you want to know? Good question.

The only answer that comes to me is nothing. He nods approvingly. I need some air, I need to think about something else for a while. I know this will go above your head, but things are really bad. We are going to have to fire Fares, he'll leave at the end of the month, Anna will start working only part time. Even with those changes, we won't make it for more than a few months, maybe until December. And that's only if nothing else happens before then. Silence. Did you see that Hrant's trial is starting back up again? Maybe Erdoğan's perpetual squabble with the Gülenists will actually lead to something, now that he's blaming them for orchestrating the murder. He opens Twitter, copies a link that calls Hrant's murder the Gülenists' "first crime," sends it to me, puts his phone back in his pocket, and then gets up as if to dismiss me. I ask when he's coming back. I don't know why, but I add that I'd feel safer if he did. This makes him smile for some reason. I'm here. He hugs me clumsily, I'm so happy to see you, he kisses me on my shoulder, along my collarbone. Then I find myself stranded in the horde of guys all busy starting their motorcycles. Erol brought out the restored collector's model from his shop window, which he's been trying to sell for months, in vain. Ten thousand lira, a motorcycle from the year he was born, 1974. The Emiratis aren't going to buy it, so I might as well enjoy it.

I make my way down the paved street toward the waterfront, having missed the last boat to the Asian side. I walk along the Bosphorus. The cruise ship port, a symbol of luxurious ambition, is in active construction; cranes stir in the night. But in front of the formerly sought-after docks, just opposite the Museum of Modern Art, there is no yacht, no cruiser, nothing. The tourists are gone, really gone. And no one seems to be asking if it's still worthwhile to remake the entire waterfront for them. Facing the cargo ships that sail silently down the strait, under the splendour of their giant shadows, I can only lament: those idiots, they don't know what they're losing. I pass the University of Fine Arts, then Fındıklı Quay, the small park where families come during the day for picnics on the waterfront. You can see dolphins from here, the kids play with BB guns or jump in the water between fishing rods. At this late hour, there are still some night owls on the grass among the cats and dogs. A couple of men sleep on the benches. I settle in, too, a little farther away. I imagine it's near a spot like this that Hrant Dink and his brothers were found by the police, sleeping in their little fisherman's basket, after their parents' argument about which of the two would be stuck caring for their children. I put in my earbuds, and from stage to stage Bashung makes love, plays dead. I sink into the black water, I fall asleep.

Sara and Ibrahim pass through Istanbul only long enough to get married in a lightning-fast ceremony, a simple formality to accelerate Ibrahim's application for Turkish citizenship. The party will come later, when there's something to actually celebrate. Fed up with her life in Gaziantep, Sara, consulting neither her employer nor her husband, accepted a job at an NGO in Iraq, needing some distance from the Turkish front—at this point, even Iraq seems to her like a relaxing destination. Ibrahim can't follow her, leaving his job at the UN would hardly be reasonable. He needs a place to stay for a few days, he has an appointment at the Syrian consulate to present his marriage certificate, as well as proof of four years of residence in the territory, which, he hopes, will permit him to avoid obligatory military service—believe me, you really don't want to do your service in Syria right now. I know, Metin feels exactly the same on the Turkish side, and so far, he's been able to postpone the timeline with trips abroad, studies, fees. But now he only has one option: get out. And your boyfriend, Ibrahim asks, he's done his service? I tell him that he went through a military school, I suppose that counts for obligatory service. Oh yeah, it all makes sense now, Ibrahim nods. What does? I was wondering what kind of man could have kept up this apartment, he explains, it's obvious that an organized person usually lives here—everything is so orderly, all those storage compartments in the kitchen, the stockpiled food, tools and utensils in all sizes, even special scissors for herbs; with your mess getting in the way of everything, it looks like he's been robbed. After military school, what did he do? He didn't finish, he fled. No more questions. Ibrahim really overdid it with dinner—he bought enough food to feed ten people. Invite friends, he tells me, isn't there someone who can come share this meal with us? It can't just be the two of us. I call the neighbours, Ruqia says she's just made hummus, and Ibrahim rubs his hands together—Syrian hummus, that's perfect.

Ruqia makes no effort to hide how she's feeling, the way she looks at me makes it clear she thinks I'm doing something wrong, and finally she asks why I haven't left the apartment yet. As if I'm occupying it militarily. He didn't ask me to leave, I say, so you're waiting for him to ask you, for it to come from him? She's getting annoying. There's a free room at my place, she adds—she lives with Metin close by—you can bring your things and come live with us. He won't come back as long as you're still here, that much is obvious. I sigh. I don't want to move out, don't want to lose this view. I feel at home in this apartment, but I can see that Ruqia thinks I'm just deluding myself.

A Godard film is playing outdoors at the Bosphorus University campus; we bring a nice bottle of wine and find a spot in the grass. Subtitles in English and surtitles in Turkish for dialogue that's impossible to translate; I imagine that, in this motley audience, no one is watching the same film as their neighbour. In the middle of the screening, people start to stir, a rumour spreads: there's been an attack. Internet networks are clogged, news is hard to get—there are deaths at the airport. Planes fly in circles above. Everyone is looking up. The film is cut short. What airport. Zehra's partner works at Atatürk Airport, I send her a message to see if everything's okay. She responds immediately, thanks for your message, we're at home, but it's clear we're not safe anymore.

I want to get out of the city, I feel like I'm suffocating, and I ask Berkin if he'd be interested in coming with me to see a little bit more of the countryside; he says no, flat out, you think if I had time off I would spend it in these shitty provinces? Turkish countryside isn't sexy for me. I ask Ruqia instead, and she agrees to leave with me. We reserve two spots at a yoga retreat, rent a car, she drives toward the mountains, everything is so deserted here, but of course they've still managed to find a place for a mosque just across the way, so close it'll drive us crazy, she says, unsmiling; now it occurs to me that I've never asked Ruqia whether she's from a Muslim family, or Christian, or what. No sooner had I arrived than I began to miss the rush of

Istanbul. I'm going in circles here: gathering nuts, making tea, and when the yogi master tells me my breathing is all messed up, I tell him to leave me alone. We learn about the attack in Nice from the usual messages asking if everything's okay. I'm looking at photos of the Bosphorus Bridge, which appears the next day draped in the colours of the French flag—always this same spectacular, one-sided solidarity—when I get a message, where are you, and then another, right away, typed hastily, the soldiers are on the bridge, get cover. I write back, I'm not in the city. You? Muz. He sends me a photo taken from the patio in which I see the bridge in blue, white, and red, the same image I'd just been looking at, except in this photo I can make out tanks. Waves of catastrophic news from Istanbul crash into my inbox. The messages are unreal. Erdoğan urges people to protest in the streets. But which streets. What protest. Against whom. Maybe a Kemalist coup, yet another in the epileptic history of the Turkish Republic. Erdoğan claims on TV that the Gülenists are behind this, his same old story. Anna says that the streets of Beşiktaş are mayhem, with the police and the military attacking each other. Panicked, she ran to the home of a friend's mother and shut herself inside. Ahmet is at home in Cihangir, disgusted, this coup is fucking staged. Georgi is stuck on a patio, at a barbecue that's likely to last for some time, it's impossible to leave, they stay outside all night and watch airplanes hover over the city, flying too low. He sends sporadic messages of terror and disbelief: they are going to bomb us. Berkin, in Galata, hears unceasing calls to prayer, so loud that he can't make calls from his home. Elsa loses it: this is it for me. I'm getting out of this country as soon as possible. Zehra was at a café in the trendy neighbourhood of Nişantaşı.

No one took the news seriously, so they started to offer rounds of a cocktail they named Coup d'État. It took them a while to finally send people home, and still, several took their time to sit under the porch to finish their drinks. It was only when they saw trucks filled with cops armed to the gills that they understood. I have to wait until the next morning to get news from Metin, who had just landed at the airport with his basketball team, a dozen or so teenagers for whom he was now responsible, amid full-blown chaos. When the nationalists burst into the terminal with flags yelling *Allahu Akbar*, it was thought to be another attack, widespread panic, lots of people made a run for it. A woman cried in Arabic *Halas, halas*—did she want them to be quiet, was she surrendering, he couldn't know. Metin abandoned their bags and rented a room for the boys at the closest hotel, just before the tanks encircled the airport. In one of the tanks sat the tea vendor's son, who ended up spending the night in prison, where he'd stay for some time. He will later say he'd arrived at the airport with his squad because they were under orders, and when they saw that something seemed wrong, they turned around. It was as they were leaving that they were stopped. And when I look at images of what happened on the bridge—the kind of pure violence that civilians unleash on soldiers—I feel relieved he made it out alive at all. Yet, as with so many others, even though he swears he knew nothing and shot no one, he will have to wait months in jail for his trial. The media gives paradoxical, unreliable news. Reading French news sources, the situation seems obscure, and from reading the press you'd think it was a democratic coup d'état. This exasperates Ruqia—what's a democratic coup d'état supposed to look like, anyway?

Even among the most radically anti-Erdoğan people I know, no one is sorry that the putsch failed, but still they won't join the protests planned in the city for the next few days, despite calls for national unity and negotiations from the secular opposition, who agree to protest on one condition: that the flags bearing Erdoğan's image be no bigger than those of Atatürk. That's where we're at.

The same message: where are you? This time I respond more calmly. I ask if he thinks I should go back to Istanbul. If I were you, I'd go back to France, he says simply, I know he means it. I ask if it's terrible there. No, come back if you feel like it. We're just stuck in the same building as two madmen who are killing each other.

The anxious hearts of doves—you've probably read that expression before, it was in his last column. The subtitle: "My current state of anxiety." In the article, Hrant spoke of his indictment for having written about Turkish poison in Armenian identity that had made him a public enemy; he spoke of the fact that he'd perhaps be better off leaving the country; he spoke of the even stronger fact that he did not want to leave. Istanbul was his home. The Armenian diaspora was breaking his heart.

Erdem is back from the United States because classes at the university are starting soon and he still owes the state another year. So he came back, despite the furious repression following the failed coup—purges among professors, the stern advice of his friends, the list of worried relatives, some fired, some arrested—and despite his photo circulating in conservative papers in recent weeks. Just before he was arrested, Demirtaş, the president of the Peoples' Democratic Party (HDP) opposition party, wrote: "We have reached the point where, in Turkey, simply advocating for peace is considered a crime"; yet Erdem signed the petition started by academics for peace in Kurdistan. Unless otherwise instructed, he'll be teaching his students next week. He has only just returned to Istanbul but he's taking the time to go out for a lemonade with me, and I'm late, as always. He told the waiter, who'd been worried about him waiting, that he was fine, he had a meeting with a journalist writing about Hrant Dink. To this the waiter became alarmed, are you sure this is really the time to be bringing up Hrant? Erdem faltered and felt ashamed. This is what destroys us so deeply, he confesses to me when I arrive—fear. I find myself not sharing certain articles on social media, mistrusting my own shadow. And yeah, on the terrace of this café in Osmanbey, a few metres from the street where Hrant was murdered, Erdem looks right, left, behind me, and behind him, too. Hi eyes scan everything around us, on the lookout for eavesdroppers, or any nefarious curiosity among our neighbours. An anxious bird. When we part ways, he says two things to me. First, don't cause me any trouble with your book. Second, don't forget to have a child. Seeing my shocked expression at this, he smiles, I, too, used to believe that art, politics, and travel were the most important things. And now I'm an old man, an artist, an activist, too, maybe. But the deepest conversations I have are with my son. He's an engineer, you know. And what he does in a physics lab in the United States seems, to me, more interesting today than all the art galleries in Istanbul and elsewhere combined. I promise you.

Istanbul in September: I remember how humid the city gets as it tilts toward autumn, it's a kind of heat that goes straight to your head. I end up moving in with Ruqia and Metin, who free up a room for me in their apartment. Every day after lunch, I cross the Bosphorus by ferry to meet up with Berkin; we talk about what we've been reading, the political situation in the country, and everything he teaches me, everything I think I understand, he just as soon deconstructs. Don't be so sure of what you think you know about Istanbul, you only know certain neighbourhoods; you should try to get out of Kadıköy every once in a while. Most people aren't like us. The newer neighbourhoods, nowadays, in 2016—this Istanbul has nothing to do with the city of Greek, Armenian, and Jewish communities of the past. It signals the one to come, though we might not come to see it for ourselves. Perhaps in a future version of Istanbul, there will be no more girls who walk alone undisturbed from terrace to terrace, nor guys in skinny jeans and earrings. Gay Pride has already disappeared, really, banned because of the state of emergency, and now it'll never come back. The protest from last year was broken up by the police before giving rise to one lasting image: the Kärcher water jets forming a rainbow above the fleeing crowd. This year, helicopters flying over İstiklal and militarized roadblocks deterred most of the demonstrators. A few weeks ago, the body of a young trans woman was found burned and mutilated on the side of the road.

On the hundredth anniversary of the genocide, the Hrant Dink Foundation awarded its annual prize for the defence of human rights in Turkey to an LGBT organization. Berkin smiles, somewhat sadly, and says I hope this doesn't mean we're in the same situation as the Armenians in 1915. So: one prize for LGBT people; one for journalist Ahmet Altan, who has just been imprisoned; and another for the conscientious objectors in 2009, which the waiter at our local café boasts of having received in person, along with a hundred other anti-militarist activists. I never really had the occasion to learn more about the conscientious objectors' movement in Turkey, but I do know that in this country, where democratic tradition is confused with the cult of the army, and much to the despair of actual democrats, anti-militarist movements are one of the meeting grounds for progressives. Since I don't dare go to the Muz anymore, I decide to resume my habit of going to the bistro downstairs and try to get the barman, a conscientious objector, to talk. He pours more beer than he talks, so when I leave these interviews I'm stupidly drunk and send blubbering messages to the other. National depression isn't getting any better. The Hrant Dink Foundation awards ceremony usually takes place around the anniversary of Hrant's birth, September 15, 1954; this year it falls during the Eid holidays. On September 16, Euphemia's blood is said to overflow from her relics, and the desolate streets of Kadıköy echo with the occasional cry of a sheep being slaughtered. I want to go and see his tomb, where is it? Probably covered with roses, especially this time of year. I have in my mind these spectacular images of an immense crowd, stretching as far as the eye can see and following the coffin on the Golden Horn bridge, moving toward the old city with thousands, tens of thousands of identical signs, round and black with bilingual slogans in white letters, "We are all Hrant, We are all Armenians." I take the tram to get there. President Erdoğan will at least be remembered for this witty remark: "Democracy is like a tram: when you reach your destination, you get off." (We can't say we weren't warned.) The route that goes to Hrant's grave runs along Hagia Sophia and the Blue Mosque, surrounded by police barricades. A little further on, we pass the university, still grieving after an attack carried out by a dissident faction of the PKK earlier in the year. And then we move into conservative neighbourhoods, where you see more and more veiled women. The tram picks up speed to make the climb up to Aksaray, and then there are no Westerners at all but plenty of immigrants, Syrians, Armenians from Armenia, and the best pastries in the city. Finally the tram stops on the Topkapı plateau, facing the walls on which the Turkish government has seemingly broken its own record for planting giant flags. Women dressed in black push their children on swings; others lounge on the grass, chatting with one another. It's 30 degrees outside and I feel perfectly indecent in my short dress; seeing everyone else around me you'd think it was cooler. I feel like the public display of outside temperature should be a ruling in my favour. I put in my earbuds to discourage any comments, but it's unnecessary; in this peaceful place, indifference is the rule. And here, the entrance to the cemetery. I didn't bother to find out the exact location of the grave, I figured I'd find it easily enough. Why I always assume I'll find something easily enough, despite so many years of evidence stacked to the contrary, is a mystery. There must be an Armenian area, and clearly it's not on this side. I wander among the Ottoman tombs. Arabic writing, legible to no one. Do the Syrians in the neighbourhood at least recognize it? Not sure. Perhaps a little better than the Turks, who have been using the Latin alphabet for four or five generations now. Fethiye Çetin begins one of her books with a note about the alphabet and Turkish literacy, saying that in 1913, her grandmother wrote to her great-grandfather, who had emigrated to the United States, in the Armenian language and alphabet. When he replied, he probably dictated his own letter, in "old script"—that is, in Turkish and Arabic characters. The children had to have it read by someone who still knew the old writing, but the grandmother did not seem capable of reading Turkish in the "new" Latin alphabet either. This shows how the founding act of the Republic was carried out amid the massacre of minorities and the brutal severing of all written transmission—"can a people who cannot read their own love poems have a history made of love? I wonder what it would be like to be a German who couldn't read Goethe, or an Englishman for whom Shakespeare's sonnets remain obscure," Ece Temelkuran writes.

Impressive tombs, undoubtedly those of dignitaries, are now abandoned. There are very few visitors around, only the gardeners. One of them passes me with his watering can, then circles back to ask if he can help. I say in Turkish that I don't speak Turkish, which doesn't convince him. He asks where I come from, I tell him, he asks if I'm looking for anything, I say no—I don't want company. I think I understand that he's in the middle of saying how my Turkish is very good, but maybe what he's actually saying is that I'm very beautiful; in any case, he takes my hand, kisses it, and wishes me a good day before disappearing. I continue down the slope for a few minutes. It seems to me like the names on the tombstones begin sounding more and more

Armenian (but no, they aren't, I'm wrong), and I keep going before accepting the obvious fact that I am in the middle of a ginormous cemetery that is uniformly Muslim. Not a cross in sight, but possibly a garden shed. I peek inside to see three uniformed police officers having lunch, staring back at me, a little bewildered. I ask them where the Armenian section is, and the thought occurs to me that this might be what some would call provocation: walking around in a dress in a conservative neighbourhood and introducing myself to police officers as I'm looking for Hrant Dink's grave. But they motion gently for me to sit down next to them and share their meal, a pepper omelette, and they ask where I come from, if I'm Orthodox, I say no, so what, then, France is on strike? I answer as if the question were obvious. Nothing surprises me anymore—maybe Istanbul has made me this way. Finally they tell me it's still a kilometre or so away, go toward the water. Enjoy the walk.

Walking in flip-flops through this seemingly endless cemetery, a peaceful little bubble. Between two sections, narrow streets where cars drive too fast, and a few pedestrians, mostly men and horse-drawn carts. Here, another shed that smells strongly of sheep, some must have recently been kept there. And finally: a small church, a monastery, a forest of crosses: the Armenian cemetery. It's quiet, divided into twenty or so numbered squares, spread out on a hill planted with cedar trees. I wander around. Some gardeners work in pairs on graves large enough to fit a community vegetable garden; some work in silence, some chat, others listen to music. They straighten up as I pass by, like mongooses in the savannah. One of them, upon seeing me, puts his T-shirt back on and leaves the tomb to fetch water at the fountain. I stop him to ask where Hrant Dink is. As if we were meeting in the hallways of *Agos*. The gardener points to the entrance of the cemetery, how could I have missed it, right next to the church. He makes this exaggerated gesture as if to indicate a huge and unmissable monument. I brace myself to be humiliated. Then I think I hear him say "third square," but there's nothing special at the third square, just more gardeners. I ask again where to go, and this time they don't just point me in the right direction but accompany me as a group, watering cans in hand, and drop me off at the third grave from the entrance. Indeed, it is hard to miss. A column and a bust of Dink in white marble, flanked by two somewhat abstract sculptures I don't immediately recognize. Behind it, a panel is engraved with Orthodox crosses and birds. Doves, no doubt in the sculptor's mind, or the seagulls that trail the ferries on the Bosphorus and can be seen behind Hrant in one of the most famous photographs of him. Or perhaps those famous pigeons whose anxious hearts thrummed in unison with his own. A poem at his feet, in Turkish. A photograph, an incense burner, a rose bush. I step back to sit down on the bench on the other side of the path, where an olive tree enters my field of vision, it's planted right in front, bent slightly from the wind, and the two sculptures that frame Hrant's face: more doves. I've never seen such an accumulation of symbols of peace: here is the grave of a man labelled an enemy of the Turks and who said, as if in prayer, don't worry, for although it is true that we have our eyes turned toward this land, it's not to take it back, but to rest more deeply within its depths.

On the plateau overlooking Maçka Park, there is a large esplanade with a statue that faces the illuminated city. Guests crowd into a fancy concert hall, where I find Erdem, dressed in his Sunday best and looking a little sad that the room isn't fuller. People are afraid to be seen here now. A video shows Hrant at an awards ceremony in Germany. His face looms large on the screen as he harangues us, his words hammering home, his fist clenched, and a quote splayed across the screen: "Turkey is not a dark country." He speaks off the cuff, just says what's in his heart and takes his bow, applause erupts and he leaves the stage, forgetting his statuette near the microphone. People laugh—on the screen and in the room we're in—as we watch him running back onstage to retrieve his award, red with embarrassment and laughing heartily himself, then he's off again, clutching it tightly to his chest. The video ends, and the lights in the room come back on. The Hrant Dink Foundation awards ceremony reviews the achievements of 2016 in the ongoing defence of human rights and democracy in Turkey and around the world. The scope is broad, ranging from associations that promote gender equality in schools in the United Kingdom to the rescue of farm animals in China, even the Syrian resistance. As my attention wanders a little in the face of this endless panorama, a heartfelt on-screen tribute is paid to the Turkish people who protested the coup. I am forced to look once more at images of that night and wonder if it's a joke. Two women standing up to tanks, among dozens of belligerent faces, are supposed to represent the democrats of 2016—seriously? Next to me, Erdem remains silent. Are we really obliged to give concessions to the government? I bite my tongue. And here are the winners. For Turkey, after this apocalyptic year, the announcement is made slowly, solemnly: Diyarbakır Barosu. "The Diyarbakır Bar Association, for its impartiality, its sensitivity to human rights issues, its opposition to all forms of violence, regardless of who uses it and for what reason, to be considered a model for the region"—each word is distinctly articulated, worth its weight in innuendo, and greeted with thunderous applause.

Outside the room, foreign correspondents in Istanbul share their concerns about the future of this country. There is talk of a support committee for Aslı Erdoğan, the new darling of European media, and talk of possible actions at the Istanbul consulate—that new consul, is he more restrictive than the previous one? In the women's bathroom, seemingly forgotten on the sink, is the international award statuette, which has just been given to Theresa Kachindamoto, an activist from Malawi. I inspect this piece of wood split with an axe, the two parts still joined together by a piece of metal shaped like an *H*, or like Hrant's dead body. I handle the wood somewhat preciously, as if his spirit could appear at my touch, but instead it's Theresa Kachindamoto, just out of the stall, a huge, warm smile on her face as she apologizes and retrieves her award. Outside it's pouring rain, and naturally I have no umbrella. I run into the Kurdish singer again, arm in arm with Erdal Doğan, formerly Hrant's lawyer, now Aslı's. I can't resist, I want to get to know her, so I squeeze into their conversation, too curious to restrain myself. The singer introduces me as if I were her best friend. It's a day of big emotions for me, she says, the fact that this prize was given to the Diyarbakır Bar Association—quite a bold move on the part of the Foundation! To dare to claim justice for Tahir Elçi. All those people poised to tear apart anyone who steps out of line right now—I'll bet they'll be grinding their teeth tonight.

I nod without asking any questions. She offers to drive us back when her tiny, yelping dog attracts the attention of the cops patrolling the entrance of the parking lot. They ask who's driving, if we've had anything to drink, and the singer, brazen as ever, snaps at them dryly—relax, guys, Ramadan is over. She chuckles at her own insolence and gets in the car, saying the last thing I need is to get myself arrested on the day we're celebrating Tahir Elçi!

In 1915, rumours spread that the order to kill had been suspended in Urfa, a few dozen kilometres from the Syrian border. Survivors were deported to Aleppo, and from there, some went to Marseille, others to America. All traces were lost. Aleppo is now inaccessible, synonymous with the hell on earth that thousands of refugees flee every day, crossing in the other direction and crowding into camps on the outskirts of Urfa; but barely a hundred years ago, even twenty years ago—Aleppo was the Promised Land. How many men, women, children have been buried on the roadsides of Anatolia, on the way to Syria? Ruqia spent a few months in Urfa when she had just arrived in Turkey. Almost everyone in her building was Syrian, staying for various lengths of time in this city that, according to both the Bible and the Quran, was once home to Abraham, this city where pilgrims still come to pray by the lake and make offerings to the sacred fish. But there aren't very many tourists anymore. "Strongly discouraged for foreigners unless there is a compelling reason," the French Embassy stipulates, "due to the conflict in Syria and the clashes between Turkish security forces and PKK militants, which could cause collateral damage"—what a delightful way of putting it. I suppose this means that, in diplomatic terms, we could consider Tahir Elçi collateral damage. At least that's the official version. I remember it like it was yesterday, Ruqia says, the end of 2015 was a veritable manhunt. Syrian resistance fighters who had taken refuge here were dropping like flies. One morning, two neighbours were found decapitated. Two young men my age, in their twenties, both activists, one of whom had co-founded a news site that still exists, *Raqqa Is Being Slaughtered Silently.* I look for the account on Twitter. I've barely typed the first two words into the search bar before a slew of suggestions for jihadist accounts pops up. Some even have friendly looking profile pictures, Kalashnikovs slung over shoulders in the setting sun. I shudder with the feeling that I've accidentally dialled the number of these psychopaths. It is a failure of artificial intelligence that Twitter can't tell the difference between the verb *is* and the acronym for the Islamic State. The editor-in-chief of Naji Jerf's newspaper, *Hentah,* was also killed in Urfa. Naji was in Gaziantep at the time, waiting for his visa to leave for France. ISIS agents proved more effective than those of the administration and caught him before he could escape, shot him dead in the street with a silencer. Ruqia asks if I've ever heard of Naji, I say yes. *Hentah* in Arabic means *wheat.* She says, no wonder it landed in your furrow.

Tahir Elçi fell like a bowling pin amid all these unnoticed deaths. He was a lawyer at the Diyarbakır Bar Association. And this city, the capital of Turkish Kurdistan, was methodically bombarded by the army under the pretext of defeating the armed rebels of the PKK. Tahir was attending a news conference near the city's iconic four-legged minaret in the historic city centre, which had been damaged by gunfire just two days earlier. Demonstrators were carrying round placards, the same as those at Hrant's funeral but in colour, with red and white slogans on the photo printed in the background of the minaret's four feet, which symbolize the cultural and religious diversity of the region. Tahir was calling for an immediate end to the fighting in the city centre. "We don't want guns, clashes, or police operations here, in this place of common humanity"—those were his last words. Now, of course, the government says that his shooters belonged to the PKK, but no one believes it. Why not Gülenists, too? You can clearly see in the videos that it was the cops who shot him. What videos, I ask. It was a news conference with cameras, video recorders, iPhones, you can find ten versions of his death on YouTube if you type the words "Tahir Elçi." Journalists huddled between a van and the minaret, two plainclothes police officers with guns drawn, who are supposed to be covering them, one of the attackers running down the street, passing in front of the car, the cop shooting him at point-blank range, turning around and shooting again, the camera showing his tense face, teeth clenched, eyes closing more and more with each shot, and in the next image we see Tahir Elçi's dead body on the ground. Long minutes are filmed after the shooting has stopped, and a cop is telling everyone to stay still. He moves forward a little to see what's happening in the street. The camera films the pool of blood as it grows; no one dares to expose themselves; the body is filmed through the four pillars of the minaret, the protesters' signs still hanging upon the monument denouncing the crime of the previous day. One reads, "I've seen wars, disasters, but never such betrayal." Tahir Elçi was killed in exactly the same way as Hrant, noted journalist Cengiz Çandar, husband of Tuba Çandar, author of Hrant's biography, which serves as my bible. Indeed, Tuba Çandar quotes this prophetic text from 2003, *Message from Someone Who Already Knows*: "How similar today's Kurds are to the Armenians of the past! My Kurdish brother, do not allow them to sabotage our demonstrations or calls for peace. At the very least, make sure you do not suffer the same fate that was ours."

It is said that the third world war has already begun and that it will go down in history as the "Mesopotamian War." In France, we learned in our history books that this region between the Tigris and Euphrates Rivers, which is now divided between Turks, Iraqis, and Syrians (mostly Kurds), was once the cradle of humanity, the birthplace of culture. And in Turkish schools, the government has chosen instead to teach children that no one has ever been exterminated on these lands, even going so far as to organize a sort of essay contest on the subject. This contest would go on to attract Hrant's indignant albeit impotent anger. Sociologist Pınar Selek, writing in the newspaper *Özgür Gündem*, attempted to tell the story of these lands without mentioning the elephant in the room, resulting in a sadly parodic essay that concludes like this: "And what about the Armenians anyway? Carried away by the winds, swallowed up by the waters."

The Euphrates—*Fırat* in Kurdish, *Fırat* in Turkish: this was Hrant's "Turkified" name, the one he chose for himself during his early years as a Marxist activist, when he was made to understand that it was better to protect his family and not flaunt his Armenian identity. The Euphrates is also a character in Jean Kéhayan's book *Stateless*. It is the story of his father's escape, a fragile fifteen-year-old leaving the ruins of his family farm in which his parents' corpses were burning. "No account tells the story of a child who made his way from Kharput to the Euphrates, but it happened," Kéhayan writes. This young man who didn't know how to swim had the idea, reminiscent of a children's game, of strapping gourds around his waist to cross the river and flee, all the way to Marseille, with a passport inscribed with the purpose of the journey, written in perfect handwriting: "cannot return." The document does not say to where, but it's somewhere close to someplace to which they were never able to return.

On the Syrian side of the Euphrates, close to ISIS's stronghold, the Promethean Tabqa Dam has been damaged by U.S. bombing and threatens to dump twelve billion cubic metres of water from the aptly named Lake Assad onto the surrounding areas and their inhabitants. A few kilometres away, Russian aircraft bombed civilians in Deir ez-Zor, once home to large Yazidi and Armenian minorities; on the internet, images are circling of the river waters, reddened by the massacre. *Look at Euphrates carrying away the blood*—the title is already taken. It's a book from the late 1980s by Yaşar Kemal in which he writes about the brutality of the evacuation of Greeks from Anatolia. But it's an old story: *The Iliad* recounts that during the siege of Troy, Xanthos, the river god, exhausted from carrying corpses, enters a vengeful rage that leads him to pursue Achilles. Convinced he would die in the waters in a manner he considered unworthy, Achilles places himself under the protection of his goddess mother. Two thousand eight hundred years later, Fethiye Çetin retraces the buried history of her Armenian family in *My Grandmother*. Çetin stumbled upon the original watery grave. "My paternal grandmother threw two children into the water. They were my uncle's daughters. Their fathers and their mothers had all been murdered, and they themselves were no longer able to walk. One of them sank straight to the bottom, but the other bobbed straight back up. My grandmother pushed her head more forcefully under the water, but again the child came back up. And then, finally, the child went down for good. And then my grandmother was next. She threw herself into the waves, was swept away, and disappeared."

But why would you want to describe all this?

The Hrant Dink Foundation is based in a former Armenian school that has fallen into disuse, only a bizarrely placed stained-glass window remains intact. It is located on Papa Roncalli Street. I picture Papa Roncalli as some benevolently chubby neighbourhood pizzaiolo and wonder what he could have done that was so extraordinary to have warranted a street named after him, especially a street that could have been named after Hrant Dink. Roncalli is a pope, you idiot. The Vatican embassy is also on this street. The women who work at the Foundation are all having lunch on the ground floor in a dimly lit canteen. The police officers who provide security for the building are eating at the next table over, which feels completely unnatural, given the state of things. I listen to the women talk about the Foundation's latest projects, carried out with increasing difficulty in the current climate, collecting testimonies about the history of Armenians in Turkey. In the south of the country, there are still so many taboos. They recently interviewed a man who had just learned that he had Armenian ancestry and was wondering how he could tell his wife, as if he'd committed a sin. It's the same in my family, one of them says: after years of searching, one of my uncles finally tracked down some cousins who had been lost during the death marches, who had converted and were still living in Kurdistan. He didn't dare to contact them, preferring instead to leave them in their relative comfort. Another colleague had DNA tests done that revealed that she had Armenian origins. This ended up imploding her family, divided between those who accepted it and those who didn't want to hear about it, assuming the CIA had rigged the tests and once again succeeded in its anti-Turkish propaganda, et cetera. Fethiye Çetin recounts the story of a family who refused to accept the inheritance left by the original family of one of these Armenian children "taken" by Muslim families and asks: "After so many years, after the danger of death has passed, why are they still so afraid?"

After leaving the Foundation, I stop by Mehmet's place. He doesn't have a phone, but whenever he's there he swings open the door, his broad shoulders and two-coloured lion's mane barely contained within the door frame. He is always nursing tea, beer, or rakı, depending on the hour. Mehmet trembles a little when he smokes, and he wears a constant, gentle smile. Because he knows I'm interested in conscientious objectors, he tells me about his military service, which he sabotaged by pretending, for eight months, to have a limp in his right leg. Just talking about it makes him start limping again. Then the beginning of his career as an actor and director; he was notoriously anti-militaristic, somewhat broken by the regime—no fewer than six trials—but he keeps memories of his past life everywhere, photos are strewn across the walls, on dressers, in the bathroom. He says, you know that Turkey basically invented intersectionality, now so fashionable for European universities. In the 1980s, progressives adopted the slogan "We are not Sabiha Gökçen," meaning we didn't want a military woman as our feminist icon, especially one who was an Armenian refugee who distinguished herself by bombing the Alevi Kurds of Dersim. You should read Pınar Selek, he says, and indeed I'd been waiting for him to say it. She did her time in prison, "the insolent little Turkish girl," as Hrant called her. And when she understood that the State had decided to come after her, she took off—perhaps forever. I tell Mehmet it's thanks to her, thanks to her book *Because They Are Armenian*, that I first heard about Dink. I especially liked her insolence, as though it were some kind of obligation that came with the privileges of a bourgeois education. Her energy to break free from them, to step out of the path of the dominant class. "Learning to see and listen to the waters that carry people into the unknown, the winds that sweep away friends"—Mehmet smiles wistfully, quoting her. Another thing: Mehmet collects hippos, which is to say anything shaped like a hippopotamus. I like the roundness, he explains, stroking with tenderness the hippo ashtray I've just brought him, found in a flea market in Cihangir. He has hundreds of hippo knickknacks stacked around his apartment, which has also become the temporary home of his friend from the Caucasus whom everyone calls Princess and treats as such. She pokes her head into the room to see who it is before deciding whether she wants to sit with us. She doesn't understand a word of English, but she's a screenwriter and likely doesn't get bored watching us like a film without subtitles.

Since August, all of Mehmet's energy has been mobilized to free his friend Aslı Erdoğan, who has been accused of participating in a terrorist enterprise and trying to divide the state, i.e., of being close to the PKK, the only evidence of which is a series of articles published in the now-unauthorized newspaper *Özgür Gündem*, whose entire subscription base and support committees are now incarcerated. She faces life imprisonment in solitary confinement without parole. Mehmet spends his days at his computer, concentrating as hard as he can on writing long emails in English to all the associations, NGOs, activists, writers, and politicians whose contact information he can find. Aslı is ill, and the current conditions of her imprisonment are worsening her already fragile physical and mental state. The first hearing of her trial, at which she will be grouped with nine other *Özgür Gündem* defendants, is set for the end of December, which means she'll have to spend at least four and a half months in prison. Requests for her provisional release have been rejected; it seems that for this country at war with itself, threatened at its borders, the most imminent danger to citizens is this one small dreamer torn apart by the suffering of the world. The same prospect awaits Necmiye Alpay, who was arrested two weeks after Aslı and is being held with her. The prosecutor suspects Alpay of having turned to violent action after a long career dedicated to philosophy and the study of languages. You who love lists, Mehmet jokes, could you tell us if there are any septuagenarian terrorists who write literary blogs outside of Turkey? On Necmiye's blog, there is an essay translated into French by the author herself, entitled "The Heart, the Rose, Time, and the Mirror," which looks at five centuries of French women's poetry and begins by asking whether it was reasonable for scholars to disparage the verses of Christine de Pisan (c. 1365–c. 1430) on the basis that she had to work on commission to earn a living. Mehmet mutters, what a waste. He tries to smile but is betrayed by the uninterrupted trembling of his hands, his glistening eyes. Aslı, Necmiye, and, before them, Pınar Selek: three non-Kurdish women accused of complicity with the Kurdish armed movement. Through them and so many others, a warning is communicated to all Turks who would dare to show solidarity with the country's minorities instead of quietly enjoying their privileges and looking the other way, which is what Europe is doing as people are imprisoned left and right. The day of Dink's funeral saw the birth of the slogan "We are all Armenians," which marked a turning point in Turkey's history, a movement of solidarity that began in 2007, during the election campaign of professor and former *Agos* writer Baskın Oran. His agenda was that "Turks defend Roma, Roma defends Adyghe, Adyghe defend the unemployed, the unemployed defend women, women defend Alevis, the Alevis defend homosexuals"—and this is what Erdoğan is at war with today.

Mehmet/Sisyphus shows me a list of arrests made in recent days, which he attempts to keep meticulously updated. Among the journalists, writers, and academics who have been imprisoned, women are astonishingly overrepresented. Mehmet does not deny that they may be specifically targeted. Aslı, who has managed to get a letter to her lawyer from prison, calls herself the "witch to be hunted down." Not everyone believes she's being persecuted, and I'm advised not to be paranoid, which is an argument that, as it happens, automatically and significantly increases my level of paranoia. Aslı is a delicate, very emotional person. The fact that she was arrested after unsuccessfully attempting to raise the alarm does not seem to have had the effect of proving her right, strangely enough; she ticks all the boxes of the "hysterical woman." Abroad, however, mobilization in her favour is gaining unforeseen momentum. Her literary agent is amazed by the sudden and unprecedented enthusiasm surrounding her work. She had already been partially translated into German, Italian, French, Norwegian, Bulgarian, Arabic, and other languages, and is now attracting interest from Spain (despite it being a country known for its reluctance to translate Turkish authors), as well as Portugal and elsewhere. Demonstrations of support are multiplying, and her books are rising to the tops of bestseller lists, including in Turkey. The sounding board of our time is coming into its own: worldwide protests with the slogans #JeSuis and #IAm, the global village, social networks, online petitions. And the fact, of course, that she is a very beautiful woman, that she has the same name as the president, that she's preaching humanism without detours or aggression—all this makes her an easy icon, an almost-idol. No doubt she'll soon be criticized, no matter what she does or doesn't do, for having benefited from this halo of glory that has descended upon her.

The day before the first hearing of her trial, her face appeared on the front page of *Le Monde*: she looked serious, beautiful, captivating. The front page circulated on social media, and her Turkish friends were shocked that a paper like *Le Monde* was making such a big deal about what was happening here that they were covering it on the front page. In the photo from *Le Monde*, she is far from the frail, fragmented, broken-voiced person who would stand before the judges the next day. This was a woman who, despite her weak body, would hold her ground in court.

A delegation of French, German, and Italian authors and journalists travel to Istanbul to attend the trial. Journalists from Paris call to gather some of my first impressions, and I'm not sure what to tell them. One of them asks me, in a vaguely cynical tone I resent, if I *really* believe that our presence here will change anything. Hrant said, this guy now says to me, that "during the genocide, if the Armenians of Istanbul were saved, it was because the embassies and consulates were located in that city." But he doesn't know Hrant like I do. So I quote Aslı to him, because it seems like readers of the French press might be able to discover, through her, that there are free spirits in Turkey: "Soberly, personally, simply, I do not want to be complicit." I hear that some French journalists, who were aware of the importance of their presence, had implored their editors to let them come but couldn't get their travel expenses paid. No news of the presence of a symbol like *Charlie Hebdo*. It seems that part of the press relies on people like me to find and transmit information, and that the editors-in-chief of these newspapers—which claim to embody French freedom of expression—don't see any point in paying actual journalists to cover this historical moment in which the rule of law is giving way to arbitrariness. From their Paris offices they advise caution, suggest writing articles while advising against it, and call to ask whether it's actually safe to talk on the phone.

The weather is getting worse, it looks like it's going to snow and the wind is picking up, so intensely that the ferries might not be running tomorrow—this is bad news, the courthouse is on the other side of town, not easy to get to. You should have slept in Europe. If you'd told me that you had to be there at nine... In case of bad weather there's always the Metrobus, the inscrutable bus system that runs on a dedicated lane that feels like rolling dice every time I take it, deciphering the list of stations it serves. Could I take the motorcycle? Yeah, right. You, on a motorcycle, on the bridge in the snow, give me a break.

The Istanbul Palace of Justice is—how shall I put this—an example of architecture that doesn't mince its words. An immense, curved structure with monumental halls, winding corridors, and many floors that loom above the police barricades at the entrance. Gigantic statues glare at you as you approach the stairs. The *Özgür Gündem* trial is being held on the third floor in what turns out to be the smallest courtroom. Just a friendly fuck-you from the administration. There are a few hundred of us—Turkish and foreign journalists, supporters, the families of the nine defendants, a number of lawyers in robes who have come to gauge the mood of justice being served these days. There are thirty additional seats for the public and not a single seat more. Four of the defendants are being brought in from prison, and Eren Keskin, a regular here, has come on her own because, for reasons no one can explain, she has not been imprisoned. They had the wrong address when they went to arrest her, I'm told, and then they gave up. Apparently the same thing happened to Necmiye Alpay, but Necmiye was arrested after turning herself in to the district attorney, believing she was doing the right thing. The moral of the story is that she's just spent 136 days in prison and Eren, nada, they seem to have forgotten about her, though it must be said that she's well known to the justice system, having been tried more than a hundred times. Mehmet smokes cigarettes in the smoking area and waves to Eren through the window; they look at each other like old friends. Eren was his lawyer in another life, when he was the one facing trial after trial for inciting the population against the army. She won them all, he says proudly. I bring good luck. As we wait, tension in the room mounts and morphs into a commotion: the public is now demanding a larger room. The police officers prepare—with utmost seriousness and racial profiling, as always—a list of people who will be allowed to attend the hearing. They conscientiously note down everyone's names; some categorically refuse to be registered in this antechamber of the demise of Turkey's rule of law. You're taking us for fools, and what's next? Foreigners are given preferential treatment over Turkish journalists, and tempers are running high. A tall brunette who speaks three or four languages loses it and spits at a guard, obviously to no avail. A curly-haired woman intervenes with astonishing calm, an appeal for compassion to the stubborn police officer, to his feelings as a father, as a fair and hard-working Turkish man. The doors open. The journalists who have been turned away question one another. A few deputies from the Kemalist party have come and are making statements rather than listening to what's happening inside, where, apparently, a show of force by the bureaucracy is being prepared. A lawyer comes out of the room furious, saying that only Aslı and Necmiye have been released from prison. Rumours are spreading that two boys are stuck in the snow, that there is no van available to bring them, and that one of them is in bad shape after being tortured and cannot be shown to the press, though later I will be told this wasn't true—they were beaten but not tortured. And this is how the trial begins, without the presence of the defendants, the two newspaper editors being accused of seeking to destabilize the state. The reading of the indictment takes forever, a war of nerves now underway.

In one of the columns published in *Özgür Gündem* for which she is being prosecuted, Aslı writes about a winter day two years ago, probably one like today, no doubt rainy, at the opening of the trial for the accomplices of Hrant's murderer. Three women were waiting outside the courthouse in the early hours of the morning, wearing photos of Hrant on their lapels. A man walked past them, identified "the Armenian who was murdered," and blurted out, "Good riddance!" Hrant was no stranger to the courts, having come several times to support colleagues who had fallen victim to the nationalism of the early 2000s, and who were embodied by a single number: 301, the article of the penal code punishing insults to Turkish national identity. Hrant was present at the trial of Elif Shafak, the bestselling author prosecuted for having referred to the "Turkish butchers of 1915" in her novel *The Bastard of Istanbul*—which incidentally featured a caricaturist who was himself accused of denigrating Turkish national identity. To my knowledge, this is the only example of a trial in which an author has been held accountable for the words of a character. The novel also ridiculed the Armenian diaspora and its ignorant hatred of Turkey. A few months later, Orhan Pamuk appeared in court, prosecuted under the same Article 301 for having stated in an interview: "One million Armenians and thirty thousand Kurds were killed on this land, but no one else dares to say so." Perhaps no one dared to say so because, as Hrant predicted, "there is a shared conviction that the price to pay, in some cases, can be worse than a criminal penalty." Orhan Pamuk's trial—which received extensive media coverage due to the celebrity of the author, a future Nobel laureate—was cut short, thanks to international pressure, and ultimately he wasn't convicted. Hrant's presence at Pamuk's trial was an epiphenomenon that went unnoticed by the press but not by nationalists, nearly sparking a riot. Fascists turned out in large numbers and forced him to leave the courthouse, demonstrating their position of strength—if not in front of international cameras, then at least to the Turkish people. Shortly afterwards—each season during the 2000s bringing its own share of 301 trials—the writer Perihan Mağden was prosecuted in turn, for once unrelated to Armenians, and instead for having defended conscientious objection in an editorial. Hrant had also come to show support, but, recognizing the same agitators who had attacked him at Pamuk's trial and not wanting to give them any excuse for another stunt, he left of his own accord, afraid his presence would harm the defendant, and apologized profusely to her. A few weeks later he himself appeared in court, also charged under Article 301. Perhaps because each of the previous trials had ended in dismissal, no one came to support him. "I wonder why my own trial didn't receive the same sensitivity and attention as the others. I absolutely must know the answer to this question," Hrant wrote. Whether by cause or coincidence, the proceedings ended in a term of six months in prison in Hrant's case, which involved a convoluted sentence about Turkish poison in Armenian blood. He crossed the line again, telling *Reuters*: "Of course 1915 was a genocide. The bottom line is that people who had lived on these lands for four thousand years completely disappeared." For these comments, which were reported in *Agos*, in *Radikal*, and in *Milliyet*, only *Agos* was prosecuted. Why? *I must absolutely know the answer to this question*—and several years later, Pınar Selek responded to Hrant, as if it were obvious, on the cover of her book: *Because They Are Armenian*. Ararat Dink represented his father in court posthumously for this final trial and received an even harsher sentence than the one imposed during Hrant's lifetime: a one-year conditional sentence in jail.

I ask a lawyer who is waiting around with us whether we—we who are trying to relay Aslı's message to the international media—should be careful about what we say and how we say it, so as not to aggravate her case under Article 301. He laughs when I mention Article 301 and dismisses the question with a wave of his hand. For you, just be careful, especially on social media. But Aslı is already facing two life sentences, so Article 301— He doesn't bother even finishing that sentence.

Erdal Doğan, the brilliant lawyer who champions all minority causes—Kurdish, Armenian, Alevi—has the spontaneous warmth of Anatolians. Obviously I never knew Hrant, but this is how I imagine him, I think to myself as I listen to Erdal speaking to me in Turkish and waving around his huge hands. He begins to look a little sorry when he notices me losing track of the conversation. I quickly scan the room to find someone who can translate his words for me: he's saying that after exhausting all avenues of appeal in Turkey, the lawyers and friends of *Agos* got together and everyone advised Hrant to leave the country immediately, while waiting for the European Court to rule on the matter. Hrant had declared just a few years earlier, "I never thought, not even for a single day, that I could abandon my country to settle in the paradise of ready-made freedoms called the West"—but he was almost convinced. Erdal asked him to at least write about it all, about what was happening to him, about the threats, about his life that had become impossible to live in his country.

Hrant said sure but didn't seem to mean it. Erdal insisted as much as he could. As he was leaving, Hrant turned back around and hugged Erdal, promising he would write. And that's precisely what he did in his two last articles. "Why I Became a Target" and "The Anxious Hearts of Doves" ring out like words from beyond the grave of a dead man looking back on his last days. After those articles, and after his murder, especially, everyone became Hrant's best friend. But I really know, Erdal says. When we first appeared in court, it wasn't like it is now. It's almost ten years to the day after his last meeting with Hrant, and today Erdal is defending Aslı Erdoğan, surrounded by dozens of supporters from around the world. That's why I like Aslı, he says simply—she was there with us when no one else was.

There are people who are familiar with Turkish law but have not yet understood that here it's become worthless. They say a break in the hearing is mandatory every two hours and therefore there will soon be a break, but it's now been two hours twice over and the judge clearly has no intention of stopping. The defendants' testimonies and the closing arguments of all nine lawyers are still to come. Eventually some people can't take it anymore and leave for lunch, and I take this opportunity to snag the seat of a comrade who does me the favour of leaving, this place is more selective than a Parisian nightclub. I sit next to a journalist who translates what's happening for me. Aslı's closing arguments, fourteen handwritten pages read in religious silence, are passed around the room. She begins with this vow: "I will defend myself as if the law still exists." Necmiye Alpay also says some words, with a voice that betrays her exhaustion and anger after four months in detention. Then there is Eren Keskin and her provocative makeup. Someone told me that she began wearing makeup in the spirit of contradiction at a time when Kurdish feminist circles were advocating for the abandonment of certain alienating codes of femininity. Her eyes, now lined with kohl, glare at the police officer who's about to stand next to her. She makes it clear to him that he must stay in his place, and no one says a word. She has not prepared a defence statement. She simply unleashes her indignation at having once again been dragged before the so-called justice system that she no longer recognizes: I've been a lawyer in this country for twenty-five years, and I'm ashamed for us. She sits back down without waiting for questions. The judge wearily repeats to the clerk what needs to be retained from Eren's statement and we read the words, written in gold letters on the wall behind him: "Justice is the foundation of the territory."

Then it's the lawyers' turn. Nine of them take the floor. It becomes clear we're going to spend the entire evening here and there's been no break since morning; we're hungry, cold, the room is gradually emptying, translators are giving up, the judge is visibly bored and acts as if startled awake when one of the lawyers says to him, you shouldn't be so casual with justice, you too might need it someday. At this, the courtroom bursts into laughter and the judge gets angry, shouting that he is being threatened, threatening in turn to suspend the hearing. The entire room, already weary of this drawn-out confrontation, begs for leniency regarding the lawyer's wisecrack. Demirtaş, the leader of the opposition party who is also facing a series of trials these days, said meekly that he did not begrudge his judges, since he knew that in the current state of the country, it was either them or him. The judge in charge of the trial of the police officers involved in the Hrant Dink case had just been dismissed from his post, accused of being too close to the coup plotters. A few days later, in *The Guardian*, Ece Temelkuran writes an op-ed called "Truth Is a Lost Game in Turkey": "This is like trying to play chess with a pigeon. Even if you win within the rules, the pigeon will clutter up the pieces, and finally it will shit on the chessboard, leaving you to deal with the mess. [...] Be warned. For fifteen years we played chess with the pigeon in Turkey, but now we don't even have the chessboard."

Against all odds—but it's only fair for arbitrariness to contain good surprises sometimes, too—Aslı and Necmiye are released on parole, pending further proceedings that could last for years. The joy that overwhelmed us at the end of the day is now dampened by the freezing rain that falls incessantly over Istanbul. At least they won't have to spend the next few weeks of this particularly harsh winter in prison. We agree to meet up for the next hearing on January 2 and promise to go for drinks together very soon.

I return home exhausted and consumed by desire for a break, to drink tea, feel a bit of warmth and quiet. My roommates have decided we'll spend New Year's Eve in the mountains, and, in any case, all the festive venues in Istanbul are on red alert, with embassies and radio stations issuing warnings to stay at home tonight to avoid a possible—no one dares say probable—attack. We rent a car and a few hours later find ourselves stranded in the snow, tires stuck, unable to put on chains, and we decide to walk the last two kilometres, guided by the GPS of our city smart phones as it gets darker. Metin keeps saying we'll be there soon and we're only 400 metres away, it's a straight shot, he says, and at the beginning we believe him, but we've been 400 metres and a straight shot away for an hour now, and it could easily be on the direct opposite side of the valley. If only we were sure of going in the right direction. Ruqia is wearing these tiny ballet flats and can't stop slipping on the ice and I can't stop laughing. We tell ourselves this could be how it all ends, our bodies found frozen on the side of the road, eulogized as three fools who thought it wise to see some nature before moving into 2017. Good riddance, as they say.

As if it's not enough to be immobilized by snow, mountain-dwellers are also deprived of electricity. It's always fascinating to see that the primary witnesses to the failure of Erdoğan—who had the nerve to make electricity his logo and name his party the "Justice and Development" party—are those who continue to vote for him most faithfully. They blame the Russians for cutting off gas supplies, suspect a possible—though unlikely—CIA conspiracy, and, more likely, the decision not to change the clocks this winter. For the first time ever, Turkey decided to set its clocks to Middle Eastern rather than European time, increasing electricity consumption by 10 percent, and here's the result: no heating other than fire, no hot water except in tea, no Wi-Fi whatsoever. We hear about the attack on Reina, an upscale nightclub, on our way back to Istanbul, thirty-nine people dead. Our apartment is also in total darkness. Metin, who's on call for his foreign clients, sits in front of his computer and responds to New Year's greetings without spoiling the mood, not daring to mention that his home is being illuminated by candles, that his cellphone is doing the work to compensate for the lack of internet, and that here we are, on the other side of the Bosphorus, counting the dead.

The next morning I return to the courthouse for the second hearing of the *Özgür Gündem* trial, and it's nothing like the first. There are hardly any attendees, very few foreigners—to the point that a witness just came up to me and asked me point-blank if I was a spy. The judge is more relaxed, and apart from an apparent and insurmountable obstacle that has once again prevented one of the defendants currently being held in the prison from appearing in court, everything seems to be proceeding almost normally. Aslı and Necmiye have nothing to add to their previous statements, and their lawyers ask, without much hope, that their passports be returned to them—but four of the defendants are already out of reach abroad with no intention of returning, and other high-profile defendants have also managed to flee, the charges against them grotesque and extremely serious—so the judge just shrugs his shoulders. The editor-in-chief of *Özgür Gündem* is also present. He's young, barely thirty, I'd say—also my age. I am told that he'd been working at the newspaper for only eight days. That makes seventeen days in prison already served for each day on duty—counting weekends. He faces life imprisonment, but what's the life expectancy in Turkish prisons when you enter them so young? The judge speaks harshly to him and uses an informal tone, which he didn't use with Aslı or Necmiye.

He calls him by his Turkish name, though we know him by his Kurdish name. The judge asks for an explanation for the books that were seized at the newspaper's headquarters, and at this Necmiye jumps up and asks to speak, saying no one "seizes" books. The judge deflects, says he's only quoting the prosecutor, and corrects an error made by the clerk, congratulating all of us now on being very careful with the words we use. The founder of the Green Party is also questioned, she babbles on about I don't know what, about Bodrum, saying she doesn't like Istanbul and wants to go home to Bodrum, as if this were a valid argument to deploy when accused of participating in a terrorist organization, but in fact this makes the judge smile, finally he cuts her off, saying we understand that Bodrum is nicer than here. We'd all prefer to be somewhere else today.

We leave two hours later with little change to the situation, a hearing before the same judge scheduled for three months from now, though neither the judge nor the defendants know whom among them will still be free in three months. We decide to walk to the *Cumhuriyet* newspaper offices, where the tea delivery man who was in police custody for having insulted Erdoğan has just been released. The police are occupying the newspaper's offices, so we crowd into the editor-in-chief's office, the former office of Can Dündar, who is now in exile in Germany and not likely to return. There aren't enough chairs, so Necmiye motions for me to sit down on the armrest next to her so she can translate. We toast to the tea delivery man who had refused to serve the president and also to the health of the journalists still in prison. A surreal photo is taken that immortalizes this moment in which drinking tea in Turkey could be considered a subversive act. The photo is then posted online, and almost immediately I receive an amused message: if you and your terrorist friends feel like drinking something other than tea, we have cold beers at the Muz.

We stop to buy cigarettes at a kiosk, and the vendor looks at Aslı for a long time with a completely impassive gaze before handing her the pack, hesitating long enough for all of us to worry that this might turn ugly, but then he makes a casual flick of his hand to signal that she doesn't need to pay, it's his gift to her. Sitting at the back of the bus, we speak English, not very loudly, but clearly the guy in front of us is listening, and the driver's eyes won't leave the rear-view mirror. A friend has loaned Aslı his cellphone until her phone line is restored, and she handles the device as if technology has made unfathomable advances in the time since she went to prison. She smiles, perhaps you will be arrested, too, for helping me. The bus drops us off in Kadıköy and we chat for a while in the square before separating. Both of us are used to walking by ourselves on cold and lonely nights—we are in our element, telling each other stories of the dancers we used to be. Aslı laughs and performs a stiff, unexpected entrechat when suddenly there appear three heavily armed, hooded soldiers around the corner. Probably a night patrol, a consequence of the state of emergency. Aslı freezes, they're coming for me, but she immediately recovers, gets hold of herself—you know when they came to my house there were dozens of them with masks, their guns pointed like this. She makes a gesture of pointing at me but just as soon changes her mind and points the imaginary gun at herself, right in the middle of her chest, chin raised. I'm going to go now, good night.

I take a few steps in the direction of home but I can't, I walk along the water, instinctively, toward the old apartment, the light's on, I ring the bell. He says no problem, come on up. I'm shaking. I inhale one whisky, then another. I send a message to Aslı to ask if she got back all right, but no response. My mouth hurts, my hands are twisted with cramps. I go to have a third drink but notice that the bottle has been confiscated. She must have gone to bed and you should do the same. I can't go to bed, I feel like throwing up, I feel like I'm caught in déjà vu but it's too late, there is nothing we can do to stop it. Stop what? Hrant's body on the ground, the white sheet lifting despite the pool of blood sticking it to the cobblestones; Naji shot dead by a silencer in the middle of the street in Antep; the two neighbours in Urfa, decapitated; Tahir Elçi running and the police officer who turns to shoot him. He says it can't be that simple. Hearing these words I'm dumbstruck, it can't be that simple, what is so simple about it, my voice breaks—but he's angry now, stop this, stop it, stop. His voice is everywhere, inside, outside, and the silence that follows is too loud, I start to cry and he goes out on the balcony to smoke. When he comes back, I'm curled under the duvet and he kneels at the foot of the bed, chin cradled in his hands. In his eyes, all the gentleness in the world. In Turkish he says, putting his hand now on my forehead, *have no fear*—the first words of the national anthem.

Ruqia works for an agency that helps Syrian refugees emigrate to the United States, but since Trump's Muslim ban, she's been temporarily laid off. She is a little dismayed—what are we supposed to do now? I propose that she interpret for me, that we go together to talk to Erdal. I ask him if Aslı is safe in the city. He hesitates. Listen, I've already lost one client, murdered in the street, what can I say? No one is safe, not her not you not me not anyone walking down the street. But one thing I know for sure: it's better to be outside than in prison. They'll execute political prisoners at the first sign of political instability.

On the day of his death, Hrant wrote: "How many of these threats are founded, how many are fantasies? I have no way of knowing. For me, the main and least bearable threat consists of this psychological torture. [...] This torture has two faces: curiosity and worry. On the one side, attention, and on the other, fear. Exactly as for a dove... About the same way as it does, I have one eye on the lookout, on my right, on my left, in front or behind me. [...] Do you know, Ministers, what it means for a man to be sentenced to the worry of a dove? [...] I know that the people of this country would never hurt a dove. Doves can live in the heart of cities, in the warmth of human throngs. Not without fear, of course, but in such freedom!" I remember having read another, less optimistic hypothesis elsewhere. Five years before Hrant reassured himself by writing that no one ever hurt the doves in this country, Murat Uyurkulak wrote: "I know that birds burn. The State makes life difficult for young people. Workers, dockers, peasants, angry minorities clash against the police. I am nostalgic for my hilltop village, my poverty, my hovel. [...] And one day, that's it. I start screaming: *Give me back my life and my honour. Give me back my masculinity, my femininity, my animality. Give me back my life, my Esmer, my Ada, give me back my mountain. Give me back my life and my bullets...* And then I go home." I wonder who would burn birds and why. Murat explains that carrier pigeons were accused of carrying messages from terrorists, bad omens of bombs. I thought that in Turkey the pigeon was associated with freedom and innocence. Yaşar Kemal, the most popular of Turkish storytellers, in one of his last texts, recounts that as far back as anyone can remember, there was a time when, on Taksim Square, in Gezi Park—which hadn't yet turned into the tomb of a teenager killed by police—street children sold birds they'd captured in Florya for a few pounds, cramming them into cages and bargaining with compassionate passersby, the birds' freedom in exchange for a place in paradise. "We didn't invent this custom, it has existed forever. Bird catchers have always captured birds and the people of Istanbul have always set them free. [...] Taksim is the busiest part of the city, and in this crowd, aren't we likely to meet a handful of people who have retained some humanity, willing to give a few coins to set these tiny, happy, proud birds free?" As we cross Taksim Square with Aslı, we run into a street vendor, I don't remember anymore what he sells. No birds, in any case, I've never seen that here. He recognizes Aslı not because he's seen her in the newspapers but because she's been here before, talked to him, given him some money, charmed him somehow, and now he says it's been a while, asks her where she's been. He also asks her for money, and even though she obviously hasn't earned so much as a penny during her four months in prison, she takes something out of her pocket. He thanks her for her kindness, says times are hard.

Yaşar Kemal's novel ends with these words: "Before me stood the symbol of Istanbul's defeat—the symbol of its insensitivity, of its forgetfulness of charity, of everything that made it what it had once been, and all it had lost: a monument made of the heads of hundreds of birds."

It's so cold I stamp my feet to feel them, the sound of the helicopter flying over us goes straight to my head. Aslı has taken refuge under an entrance a little ways off, she tries to keep a low profile, but people are recognizing her, pointing at her. Her pink hat reminiscent of those seen all over the media a few days ago at the Women's March against Trump. Gathered for the anniversary of Hrant's assassination, a few hundred—maybe a few thousand—people, battered by the cold and rain, young and old, veiled women, friendly looking Anatolians, hair dyed blue, red, henna, and two women who've just been released from prison who have come out to carry their black-and-white signs saying, "We are all Hrant," "We are all Armenians," in Armenian and in Turkish. Another sign reads: "Justice for Hrant Dink and Tahir Elçi." But in even larger letters on the facade of the former *Agos* offices, above the plaque marking the spot where he was shot, the obvious is spelled out in huge letters: "10 years without Hrant, 10 years without justice." Aslı is being bombarded by protesters who want to shake her hand, take a photo with her; she smiles, sincere and exhausted and still, I think, a little incredulous, struggling with her sudden and rather inconvenient fame. Rakel Dink takes the podium, surrounded by her children, for the tenth time on a January 19. In 2007, standing before Hrant's coffin, she released a dove that landed directly in the middle of the crowd, on the coffin, and uttered these words in her piercing voice that makes us shiver, this broken voice that has not stopped crying out since, this voice whose very existence is an act of revolt: "My brothers, if we do not question the darkness that has turned babies into murderers, we will never emerge from it." It goes without saying that we have not emerged from it. In an article from January 23, 2007, entitled "Who Killed Hrant Dink?" the *Monde diplomatique* painted an alarming picture of the situation: "Over the past fifteen years, eighteen other journalists have been murdered in Turkey and twelve are currently imprisoned." Twelve! A mere trifle when viewed from 2017. Today's figures show 146 journalists behind bars, and the number of murders and "suicides" in prison remains the blind spot of all official reports. And the trial that aimed to uncover the accomplices involved in Hrant's murder fluctuates according to the whims of political exploitation—obviously, in keeping with the times, new culprits close to the Gülen movement are being discovered. Amid this general collapse, Rakel's humanism, her indignation without hatred, seem to be the only things that have remained intact, rising above the fray, tirelessly repeating the same messages of peace. "It's not just about living together, but—and this is more important—it's about living happily and equally. And freely, and with dignity. Let us put an end to the anxiety of doves in this country." As the demonstration ends, people stick their black-and-white placards at the feet of trees, scattered, silent sentinels on both sides of the police barricades, echoing from one end of the boulevard to the other: "For Hrant," "For Justice," "We are all Armenians."

We all eat dinner in the warmth of Mehmet's house, surrounded by hippos, with the Princess of the Caucusus and Sibel, who made a short film in support of Aslı while she was in prison and, before tonight, has never had the opportunity to meet her. Sibel is nervous, talking too much. Aslı listens politely as she massages her neck, still suffering the after-effects of her time in prison; she still hasn't taken the time to see a doctor, and the cold makes everything worse. I don't know how the conversation has turned to ballet, but Aslı likes to talk about dance, and we all begin comparing the shapes of our calves to see who has best retained the traces of their ballerina training. Princess has the conversation translated because for once we're not talking about politics and she's actually interested in what we're saying—and when I point this out to her she nods and takes the opportunity to ask, solemnly, my permission to use me as a character in her next film. I grimace, because since when do you ask people for permission to use them. Sibel says it's not that complicated to change names, and Princess pouts, I'll do whatever I want.

In the taxi on the way back, it's snowing and we aren't sure whether the bridge is open to traffic. If it's not, we'll be stuck. The taxi driver tries to convince us to get out at the pier and take the ferry, if there is one, and then take another taxi once we get to the Asian side, but no thanks—it's past midnight and we have no desire to find ourselves stranded in the snow in Üsküdar. He crankily agrees to drive onto the bridge, which is, for once, completely deserted. It is lit up by this horrible red light that commemorates the night of the coup, the triumphant nation, the blood of fallen martyrs. We are driving way too fast for the snow and it's stressing me out, and once we arrive on the Asian side, the driver, no doubt eager to get rid of us, decides to take a shortcut and rushes headlong in the wrong direction on a one-way street. I let out a huff and he slams on the brakes, skids, and barely misses a pole before turning around to ask what my problem is, I point to the one-way sign and this makes him laugh, which relaxes the atmosphere a little bit. He starts driving again, waving a cute little hello to the sign and says in his best English, welcome to Middle East, milady. Aslı asks me questions about my book, I say I don't want to change the names, because a name is important, after all. I'm explaining this to a woman whose name means Authentic. She doesn't make a big deal out of it, whether about her own writing or the fact that her own image has recently completely escaped her control. She asks what he, my main character, thinks about it all.

But how is it possible that *I* be the main character in this gallery of martyrs, what am I doing here at all? I shrug my shoulders—are you asking yourself this question only as it relates to the book? He sidesteps the issue. At the end of your book, do they live happily ever, do they have lots of children? I don't hide the fact that it doesn't look good. He thinks for a moment, asks if it's really fiction, and when I say yes, we can do whatever we want, he asks, if it's at all possible, I'd really like to have a BMW instead of a Vespa.

An opposition MP currently under investigation has learned via Twitter, from sources close to the government, that he has been convicted, even though the judge has not yet handed down his verdict. Metin finds this highly comical, but Zehra says, I don't really feel like laughing anymore, for real. I ask her since when. She thinks about it, then says, ever since we saw the police posing next to Hrant's murderer with the Turkish flag. What kind of country is this, where you can murder a man in the middle of the street and then be congratulated by those who were supposed to protect him? That, for me, was the end of Turkey—the end of Turkey and the end of humour, that beautiful weapon of the poor. We *really* need help. Ece Temelkuran also regrets the lost power of Gezi's boldness, when protesters dressed up as penguins to thumb their noses at pro-government TV channels that broadcast animal documentaries so they wouldn't have to cover the ongoing revolution: "At the time, it seemed like an extremely powerful and subversive mode of resistance. But little by little, this humour became sarcasm, so systemic that it became a way of thinking. That's when we lost our seriousness in this fight. And now there's nothing left to laugh about."

I disagree with this last idea, now reading the plea of journalist Ahmet Altan, accused of sending subliminal messages (yes, reading the indictments these days is anything but boring) to the coup plotters. He currently faces three life sentences—and has also been found guilty of complicity with the PKK, among other things—which is serious enough to dispense with the pathos. Due to the author's celebrity, his plea, prepared in prison and now due to be read in court, has already been published in Turkish, translated and printed in English, distributed to journalists and posted online and translated into other languages, including French on the *Kedistan* website. Since we must find some interest in the "judicial pornography," as Ahmet Altan calls it, which the regime has been feeding us for months, the prospect of seeing some of this country's most brilliant writers, intellectuals, and polemicists take the stand promises to be memorable. Ahmet Altan settles his score with the bureaucrat who took it upon himself to draft the indictment against him. In a show of rhetorical swagger, Altan begins: "It is being claimed that I discredited the investigation by saying that there is no 'freedom of thought.' Let me first break the bad news to the prosecutor: your investigation has no credibility. Not in Turkey nor anywhere else in the world. [...] Look at the number of times I spoke to Ekrem Dumanlı, and if that number is higher than the number of times Ekrem travelled on Tayyip Erdoğan's plane, then we can perhaps discuss whether or not talking to Dumanlı is a crime. But if Dumanlı has spoken to Erdoğan ten times more than he spoke to me, don't bother me with this nonsense. [...] I love it when such vague, empty, and useless statements are paraded before us under the guise of the law! [...] I couldn't care less about your prison. [...] I am not the kind of man who will act cowardly and waste the decades already behind me out of consideration for the years ahead of me."

Zehra does not share my enthusiasm for this—she's annoyed by the cockfight. It's like that megalomaniac

Demirtaş (the boys at the bar whistle in unison when they hear criticism of the opposition leader who's usually always at the Muz); since he's been in prison, it seems he can find nothing else to do but write romance novels. As if one could still afford to write romance novels! I try to find some of these stories online, the romances the alleged terrorist Demirtaş is ostensibly writing from his prison cell. I am consoled about the violence done to these enlightened and sensitive individuals by telling myself that Turkish prisons have never been as well attended as they are today, so they are probably home to the most sophisticated literary salons in all of Istanbul. There's a joke going around that a prisoner asked the prison library for a novel by Ahmet Altan, and the guard came back empty-handed, saying the novel in question was not available, but he could just talk to the author, who was a few cells away. I, too, am looking for the novels of Ahmet Altan available in French, and it turns out that he, too, has tried his hand at romance novels. I find one called *Love in the Time of Revolt*. I agree with Zehra on at least one thing: it's a cheesy title. She sticks her tongue out at all the boys, Berkin says, I must not understand your book at all, then—I thought this was precisely your subject.

Armenian MP Garo Paylan was expelled from Parliament for uttering the g-word. A void is forming around the HDP opposition party, many of whose elected representatives are currently in prison and staging hunger strikes to protest the conditions of their detention. HDP representatives have been stripped of parliamentary immunity—to the vast indifference of their opposition and European colleagues—and thrown into prison, and will soon be stripped of their mandates, too, to ensure that from the depths of their cells they cannot interfere with the referendum vote that is set to give President Erdoğan full powers. Garo Paylan is one of the few who has not been arrested, at least not yet, so he was sitting in parliamentary meetings, during which it is no longer unusual for MPs to come to blows. Garo made a speech calling for calm, recalling the devastation that nationalism had already wrought in this country. "Between 1913 and 1923, we have lost four peoples: Armenians, Greeks, Syriacs, and Jews. They were deported amid massacres and genocides on a massive scale." The forbidden word had its effect, and he was excluded for three sessions. This is obviously completely arbitrary, it's not even the first time he has used the word in this chamber, but now, who knows why, it didn't go down well. I notice that, apart from him, we don't hear much about Armenians in the ongoing repression. *Agos* is not particularly involved. Yetvart Danzikian, who took over as editor-in-chief after Hrant and

Etyen Mahçupyan (the latter of whom never hid his sympathy for Erdoğan when he embodied the "Muslim democracy" option), confirms that they're no longer on the front line—since Hrant's death, the authorities have left *Agos* relatively unbothered. In 2017, it's undoubtedly a national symbol, but above all it's a newspaper with a circulation of a few thousand copies, dedicated to community affairs. Even if, of course, we stand in solidarity with our colleagues who are being targeted, Danzikian tells me cautiously— Then he stops himself. I know that Hrant wouldn't have shared this restraint, he who said that "presence and initiative are all the more necessary when dialogue is not taking place; if we exist, it's today that we must *show up*"—but now Hrant is dead, and no one wants to die in his place.

"The sacrosanct dialogue promoted over the past ten years is insidious," Ece Temelkuran corrects, for she has learned her lesson. We are told that we must engage in conversation with people from the other side, that we must let them express themselves, we must understand them. But the problem is that the other side has no intention of talking to us. So, in every case, dialogue boils down to the fact that we must respect them. I wonder if we should instead try to understand ourselves, talk more among ourselves first—and by *us* I mean: people capable of critical thinking. In this completely tense moment, the essayist renowned for her political analysis is reluctant to take refuge in fiction, seeking other languages so as not to break off the conversation. "I am trying to be the one who tells the story without taking sides, who tells the story in its entirety. Because if you tell it from only one point of view, you don't hear the other side, and, more seriously, they no longer hear you."

Berkin works for this new online media outlet, which,

in just a few months, has become a benchmark for independent journalism in Turkey at a time when all traditional sources of information have collapsed. They have set up their offices in a warehouse in a dreadful, semi-new neighbourhood, where the highway curves between towers covered with giant advertisements, if not election banners. The editor-in-chief, a figure in investigative journalism who struggles to reap the rewards he deserves for being one of the first to expose the explosive alliance between the AKP and the Gülenists, gives me a somewhat cold reception because he's sick of Western voyeurism, you want to know something? Are we under pressure? The answer is no. We're just doing our job. I am not, and I do not want to be, a soldier for freedom of expression. I just want to be a journalist, a good journalist who has now invented a media outlet that is unique in the world, a new information tool that has been adapted to social media. That's what we're doing here, and that's what should interest you. I'd rather see investors coming in here instead of this daily parade of foreign colleagues who ask, always with a touch of Orientalism, what they can do to help us—we don't need any help, just money. Berkin says that's a bit much—that international support, even if largely symbolic, doesn't hurt, you yourself went to interview *Charlie Hebdo* after the 2015 attack. Here Ruşen switches to French, which he speaks perfectly. While he does not want to play the role that the world expects of him, he willingly agrees to talk about the man he can no longer call his friend—after his death, he reasons, too many people claimed to have been lifelong friends with him, part of his inner circle; all I will say is that we knew each another, and I liked him. As terrible as it may sound, Hrant's death opened up something, a window of opportunity that could have been a path of redemption for Turkey. The country was forced to discuss certain issues, ease tensions. And this window of opportunity has been closing before our eyes for several years now—even faster, and more dramatically, in recent months—trapping all those who rushed into it, whether naive or clear-headed, in a dead end; but that's how it's been for a long time, playing yo-yo with fate in this country. Now, you Europeans: what is *your* role in this?

In an interview filmed in 2005 by a French television network in his *Agos* office, Hrant speaks to Frédéric Mitterand. The walls are covered in photos, and Mitterrand says he counts two photos of Atatürk, how they are surprising to find here, these images of an icon of Turkish nationalism. I catch a hint of mischief in Hrant's eyes, sparkling beneath the seriousness that overtakes the controversial nature of the question. "I chose a photo of Atatürk as an intellectual; that's the side of his personality I prefer," he said. "I put it up myself, no one forced me to." A wave of his hands indicates that he doesn't care whether or not he's believed. "The Armenian catastrophe has been buried under the founding measures of the Republic, and to question the narrative of what happened is an attack on Turkish identity, it seems to me." (At the time of this interview, Hrant was already facing two lawsuits for insulting national identity.) Since the beginning of the Republic, he continues, it has always been difficult for peoples to live in Turkey, not only for Armenians: he goes on to list the litany of difficulties experienced by Alevis, Muslims, Kurds, then goes on to talk about the European Union—that's why we want to join the Union, he says, because we have this urge toward democratization. Not just for Armenians, he insists, weighing his words, opening his hands: for all of us. Frédéric Mitterrand insists on the word *genocide*. Words are important, he asserts—this attempt to corner his interlocutor is met with a shrug—so, genocide or massacre? Hrant rejects those who want to have the genocide recognized abroad as well as those who deny it in Turkey. "Both are extremely harmful to the people who live here in Turkey, and to Armenians in general, whose tragedies are used for political ends that do not concern them, that do not solve any problems, that do not heal any trauma. We should not allow this exploitation to continue." And two final questions from the interviewer: Are you alone? Are there a lot of people who think like you? Once again, a solemn combination of gravity and generosity in Hrant's voice as he melodiously articulates a long Turkish word: "I can't know that. My ideas are probably a little romantic. But inch'Allah, God willing, everyone thinks like me."

Die and we will love you, goes a popular Armenian proverb. "The same people who today, after his death, attribute to him all the virtues of a courageous intellectual, and even make him the symbol of their long-standing cause, were not nearly as enthusiastic when he was alive," writes Jean Kéhayan, in the preface of a book by Hrant that was rejected by his publisher during his lifetime, in which he closes once and for all the door on any bitterness: "My curses are directed at the past."

On the radio, Wajdi Mouawad recounts the legend of the amphibious bird who circles above a lake. Fascinated by the fish, the bird dives in. It should drown, but it escapes death because its desire for the other, its curious empathy, is stronger than the laws that dictate that birds live in the air and fish live in the water. I fall asleep listening to the segment, and in my dream flocks of birds fly over a lake. I float on my back, watching them as they circle around me. I wake with a start to discover, across my stomach, a huge scar that has opened, now my guts are spilling out into the sea, attracting the hungry birds.

Even side by side, the most parallel paths don't end at the same time. In a drawing by Reiser, *The Bridge of Lost Children*, a broad-shouldered figure holds a child's hand to cross the bridge, which is only wide enough for one person at a time. From the footprints in the snow behind them we can see that two small feet have already fallen into the abyss. Karin Karakaşlı says that one day, when the death threats were raining down on Hrant, she was told that if she didn't want to walk beside him in the street, she didn't have to.

The multinational company that employs Metin offers him a job in London—terrible pay, but he accepts without a second thought—and Ruqia decides to join her sister in Germany, where she has taken refuge with her children. The apartment is going to be returned to the owner, and Metin discourages me from staying there, you won't find anyone to pay the rent with you, the people you'd like to live with, all of them are getting out of here. "No one abandons their home without reason," declared Patriarch Bartholomew in the early 2000s, lamenting the almost total disappearance of the Greek community in Turkey following decades of oppression. "We're tired of living in the land of dead doves," sighs Ece Temelkuran. A journalist friend agrees to meet up with me—somewhere other than the Muz, her usual haunt—and she seems nervous. She says I think that once fear has taken hold, the only thing left to do is leave. The reason I've stayed until now is that I have a Bulgarian passport and I knew I could leave when I'd had enough. An ironic, cruel, bitter smile—you'd have to be blind not to see that they're going to destroy everything. And it won't be the first time. Here history repeats itself ad infinitum, we have a culture of tabula rasa; everything is always rebuilt on the ruins of the previous era. They will leave nothing of the Istanbul we knew. I look at her and don't know what to say.

Berkin's green eyes and long, dark eyelashes growing from the edge of this oasis—he would be almost intimidatingly handsome if it weren't for his friendly lips and warm smile, quick to appear at all times. I tell him that my residence permit has expired, and that in times like these it's better not to get involved with the cops. He nods in agreement. We'll continue our project via email. He's not worried, once it's all under way I can send you the drawings at my own pace, we'll go back and forth, it'll get done. He's not holding me back, I point out. He smiles quickly, tenderly, I'm not going to ask you to stay for me, after all. I'm a little tired of crying over nothing when I shouldn't and not crying when I should, but I feel it coming on again. I try not to say anything. Berkin looks at me. Sweetheart, it's time we hug now. What can I do for you, you want some MDMA? Oh no, please. You're wrong, it really helps with introspection. With friends like these I might as well kill myself right now—and, I ask him, who would ever believe I need more introspection in my life? Berkin stands up, grabs my chin, kisses me on the mouth, just the lips, it's going to be okay. An immense tenderness overwhelms me, softens me, relaxes me long after he's gone.

Why are you making that face? I'm leaving. He smiles and recites in Turkish a verse from Cemal Süreya that everyone learns at school: "You're leaving, and what about your eyes?" I know the answer: "They're leaving, too." And I feel like the door is closing behind me. How many years have we known each other, he asks, you've always just come back. But now, sincere laughter at my utterly desperate expression: Cut the crap, woman—you chose this life. You're like Hrant now, a worried pigeon. You're going to take a trip around the world and come back to Istanbul, you're not done with us yet. And if Istanbul is destroyed? And if Istanbul is destroyed, at least you won't have done all this for nothing—the book, I mean. It's true that at least these voices from Turkey that I love so much won't only be in my head. And you? What will you do? He takes the question seriously; he's really thought about it. Why not Beirut. Or even further away from this mess—Buenos Aires. I add Marseille. Marseille, of course, except that it's Schengen. But really, I don't think any of them are going to succeed in making me dislike that place.

As I wander the streets of Cihangir for a final farewell stroll, I run into Necmiye Alpay, walking with determination, her hands clasped around the straps of her backpack, wearing a summer dress. She looks like a child rushing to school. I call out to her, pulling her out of her thoughts.

She hesitates, and I ask in French if she recognizes me. At this, a huge, warm, delighted smile spreads across her face. She goes on in French, compliments me on my dress and I hers, I could talk to her about anything and everything—her laughing eyes are basically begging for it—but she's already running late. If you don't mind, she says tentatively, embarrassed perhaps by her own politeness, I should go. I ask if she's going where I think she's going, to the gathering of Kurdish mothers that takes place at the end of the street every Saturday, and she nods and laughs: Exactly! I tell her I hope she can take a vacation soon, perhaps abroad, if her passport is returned to her soon. She replies, more seriously now, I don't see why I should leave. I did nothing wrong. She bounces away and I stay still.

In the words of Alsı in the *New Yorker* earlier this week: "Whether you like it or not. I am Turkey. Whether you accept it or not, we [the journalists and writers] are the language and the conscience of this country."

"I sing, without hope, on the boundary." Sarah Kane's last words roll around my head as I make my way through the airport. Security measures have been tightened at the entrance to the terminal, where two security guards were shot dead in a Kalashnikov attack just six months ago. This is where, on the night of the coup, Metin hid with his basketball team as a terrified woman shouted at Erdoğan's supporters, *Halas, halas!* It was also here that the tea vendor's son was arrested, the last time he exerted his free will—but too late, bad move—and now it's likely he won't see the Atatürk airport terminal before doing a few years in prison. Nor will those banned from leaving the country—and the same goes for the growing number of people who are banished from Turkey. I think of Fethiye Çetin's grandmother, who hid using a fake identity during the genocide and spent her entire life without a passport, never daring to ask the authorities for papers. And Hrant, who did not get his first passport until very late, in 2001—suspected of belonging to a pro-Armenian terrorist organization, or simply as an Armenian, or for no reason at all, he had to wait forty-eight years before obtaining permission to leave Turkey, at about the same time he was being inundated with calls to leave, it was now or never. Then he wrote a biting article in *Agos* called "I Was the Only One Missing": "If we absolutely must find reasons to be hopeful [...] allow me to share with you a development that affects me personally. [...] For reasons unknown to me, until today, I have never been able to obtain a passport. [...] I have now finally obtained satisfaction, and all injustice done to me has been redressed. Don't ask me why this good news is not included in the EU reports!"

He took advantage of it, of course. He was invited to give lectures in the United States and Europe, already an important figure to the Armenian community, one of the few Armenians in Turkey to speak out loudly and clearly. He came once to Marseille at the invitation of Jean Kéhayan, and it seems that his meeting with the diaspora there caused quite a stir. Nervous, on the eve of his first trip, he went to the airport to go through security just to see if they'd really let him leave the country.

I might have considered doing the same, because as I head toward the border police it feels like I'm playing a game of heads or tails. I have a list of numbers saved in my phone to call in case of trouble: lawyers, activists, journalists, organizations and associations that help people who fall prey to the Turkish state's paranoia. No one has been able to tell me for certain if I'm actually at risk; some frowned looking at my Twitter account—damn, you really should've been more careful—as well as some random articles published online, asking why I'd published them under my name. Others believe that, given my contacts, I am bound to be under surveillance anyway, and yet more others shrugged, thinking the Turkish police have other priorities at the moment and that, at worst, they'll be delighted to see me leave. To make matters worse, I've greatly exceeded my residence permit. All to say that I'm unlikely to go unnoticed. My luck is that there have been these massive purges of civil servants, so customs officers are understaffed and, most of the time, overwhelmed. Despite the paltry turnout, there is a queue at the checkpoint, and they are trying not to fall too far behind. I stand in line behind a family with two little girls, one of whom is whimpering, and the father, already carrying a heavy load, sweeps her into his arms without complaint. From behind, he looks like Naji Jerf, his hair, his height, his shoulders pushed back. The satisfied child looks at me over her father's reassuring shoulder, her hand clutching a keffiyeh. Once upon a time, or maybe not, Hrant stood here clutching his new and precious passport, poised to hand it to a customs officer. And there were also Pınar Selek and Can Dündar, embarking on what might be definitive exile, realizing there'd be no justice for them in Turkey—only prison, torture, maybe murder. Naji never set foot here at all. I stare down at my feet, the sticky linoleum. I think of the *Charlie Hebdo* offices flooded with the blood of friends; it's been a long time since I've thought about that. The unbearable furrow. Other travellers gather behind me, from everywhere, Anatolians, black ghosts from the Gulf, Asians. Women in chadors mechanically lift their veils under the indifferent gaze of the police, who have to repeat their request when a veil is lowered too quickly for them to see properly. You can immediately recognize the men who have come to Turkey to have hair implants, it's cheaper here; they look like they've been literally scalped, their skulls raw. Now it's Naji's turn to step forward with his children, his arms full of luggage. He must have all his papers in order, he doesn't seem stressed, and the child in his arms keeps her eyes on me until the customs officer lets them through without further questions.

Now it's my turn. The bored inspector looks at my photo, all the stamps; he raises his eyebrows, scans my passport, checks the screen, picks up the phone, tells a colleague he's sending him a French woman, hangs up, directs me to the police office. I send a message to Ruqia: Bingo, I'm with the cops. I choose to approach the officer who seems to me the friendliest looking and act as if everything is normal, I put down my bags before handing him my passport, phone in hand, incoming messages from a worried Ruqia. I see the police officer scan my passport again and print out the total length of stays in the country as I sneak a text to Ruqia saying it's nothing, just the visa. The agent asks what I'm doing in Turkey. Tourism. I try to say it without sounding rude, but he rightly points out, you've been doing tourism for the past year and a half? I correct myself: I'm in love. With Istanbul. His face goes blank. He asks where I lived, why that neighbourhood, how much was my rent. How did I spend my days. Yoga, I tell him, I've been doing yoga. I hope he doesn't think I think he's a fool. He gives me a fine and tells me that if I don't want to pay it, I'll be banned from the country—does that interest me? I see my whole life flash before my eyes. I shake my head no. He looks even more perplexed as he hands me the bill.

I return to the previous checkpoint, this time everything is in order and I'm officially out, nothing left for me to do now but die of longing. My ears ring with the words of Aslı, who would go into exile just a few weeks later: "Even though I'm leaving, this city of seagulls and boats on the Bosphorus will obviously continue to grow, live, and die somewhere on earth." At the boarding gate, I am reunited with Naji and his children, the little one asleep in his arms, the older one playing beneath the seats. So he's flying to Marseille, too, after all. I sit down on my bag nearby and stare at this family waiting to board. I put in my earbuds to drown out the noise of the living and the dead, of the Vercors, of the depths of the coves, and Bashung sings, *In my boots are mountains of questions / where an echo of you still remains.*

Dear future, I am ready.

ACKNOWLEDGEMENTS

This book couldn't have been written without the chain of solidarity that was created over many months, which surrounded, guided, and often provided shelter for me, from Marseille to Istanbul, Ankara, Fethiye, Antep, and Urfa. There are many people who inspired the characters in this story, which is also their story: Merve, Muhammed, and the "professional quitters"—Derya, Melike, Nadia, Zeynep, Helena; in Kadıköy, the "Recaizadeliers"—Julie, Korhan, Kat, Marsel, Zeki, Mazo, Melih, Aline, Sasha; from one bar to the next—Selin, Ozan, Anne, Beril, Quentin, Fiona, Daphné, Wendy, Emmanuelle, Laurent, Serena, Lülü; at Mehmet's apartment—Alexandre, Javier, Princess, Nilay, Adar, Erdal, Aslı. With gratitude to Patrick for the hotline; to Laurent and Pascal for the hospitality; to the Marseille crew—Léo, Manu (and Mona), Joanne, Laure, Yamina, Emmanuel (and Baby Jacob); my hysterical witches—Marie, Cath, J.P.; Daniel and Daniela; Isabric and Les Mougenettes; the Aponia dream team, the Fs—Mehtap, Efe, Ozan, Liudmyla, Fatih.

To those I asked to speak about Hrant, whom it would be irresponsible to name here given the current climate—I'd like to express my gratitude for your unwavering kindness, as well as my hope that I've not betrayed your trust. I'd also like to thank Mehmet Atak, *çok değer verdiğim arkadaşim*, Jean Kéhayan, Cengiz Aktar, and Necmiye Alpay, who were kind enough to be early readers of this book.

The Furrow is dedicated to those whose absence and memory reverberate beneath every word.

REFERENCES

ALPAY, NECMIYE.

"Was Hrant Dink an 'enemy of the Turks?'" *Yaklaşma Çabası* (blog). 2010.

"Les femmes poètes francaise, ou le cœur, la rose, le temps et le miroir." *Yaklaşma Çabası* (blog).

ALTAN, AHMET.

L'Amour au temps des révoltes. Translated by Alfred Depeyrat. Actes Sud, 2008.

"Acte d'accusation ou pornographię judiciare." *Kedistan*, July 15, 2017.

ÇANDAR, TUBA.

Hrant Dink: An Armenian Voice of the Voiceless in Turkey. Translated by Maureen Freely. Transaction Publishers, 2016.

ÇETIN, FETHIYE.

My Grandmother: An Armenian–Turkish Memoir. Translated by Maureen Freely. Verso Books, 2012.

COPEAUX, ÉTIENNE.

"Les colombes inquiètes." *Susam-Sokak* (blog). June 27, 2012.

DEMIRHISAR, DENIZ GÜNCE.

"Emotion and protest in Turkey: what happened on 19 January, 2007?" *Open Democracy*. January 28, 2016.

DINK, HRANT.

Chroniques d'un journaliste assassiné. Edited by Günter Seufert. Translated by Haldun Bayrı and Marie-Michèle Martinet. With an introduction by Karin Karakaşlı, translated by Bernard Banoun. Galaade, 2010.

Deux peuples proches, deux voisins lointains: Arménie—Turquie. Translated by Emre Üler and Dominique Eddé. With a foreword by Etyen Mahçupyan and a preface by Jean Kéhayan. Actes Sud, 2008.

"Hrant Dink & Frédéric Mitterrand / 24H à Instanbul." Youtube video, posted by HAY prod 2, January 24, 2015, 14 min. 12 sec.

ERDOĞAN, ASLI.

Le silence même n'est plus à toi. Translated by Julien Lapeyre de Cabanes. Actes Sud, 2017.

Le Mandarin miraculeux. Translated by Jean Descat. Actes Sud, 2006.

"Nous avons laissé derrière nous une trace profonde, invisible." *Babelmed.* February 1, 2007.

Lettres de prison. Compiled by *Kedistan.* December 2016.

EUROPEAN COURT OF HUMAN RIGHTS.

Opinion concordante de M. le juje Sajó à laquelle Mme. la juge Tsotsoria déclare se rallier (Dink v. Turkey), Judgement, 2010 Eur. Ct. H.R. (Sept. 14).

GÜNDAY, HAKAN.

Encore. Translated by Jean Descat. Galaade, 2015.

JERF, NAJI.

"ISIL in Aleppo." Youtube video, posted by FreeSyrianTranslator, April 3, 2016, 24 min. 49 sec.

"Naji Jerf." Youtube channel, joined December 21, 2011.

KÉHAYAN, JEAN.

Mes papiers d'Anatolie. Éditions de l'Aube, 2006.

L'Apatrie. Parenthèses, 2000.

KEMAL, YAŞAR.

Alors, les oiseaux sont partis... Translated by Münevver Andaç. Gallimard, 2010.

PAYLAN, GARO.

Quoted in "HDP MP Mr Garo Paylan Was Suspended From The Parliament for 3 Days." *Peoples' Democratic Party*. January 16, 2017.

SHAFAK, ELIF.

The Bastard of Istanbul. Viking, 2006.

SELEK, PINAR.

Parce qu'ils sont arméniens. Translated by Ali Terzioğlu. Liana Levi, 2015.

Verte et les oiseaux. Translated by Lucie Lavoisier. Illustrated by Elvire Reboulet. Éditions des Lisières, 2017.

SOYSAL, AHMET.

"Prononcer aujourd'hui le très ancient nom." *Critique* 543-544 (1992).

TEMELKURAN, ECE.

Turkey: The Insane and the Melancholy. Translated by Zeynep Beler. Zed Books, 2016.

Deep Mountain: Across the Turkish–Armenian Divide. Translated by Kenneth Dakan. Verso Books, 2010.

"Truth is a lost game in Turkey." *The Guardian*, December 15, 2016.

"Ece Temelkuran on Hard Talk Full Version." Youtube video, posted by Ece Temelkuran, October 10, 2016, 24 min. 24 sec.

TURKISH CLASS 101.

"İstiklal Marşı — The Turkish National Anthem." Turkish Class 101. November 4, 2022.

UYURKULAK, MURAT.

TOL. Translated by Jean Descat. Galaade, 2010.

Invisible Books produces fine Canadian literature for those who enjoy such things. As an independent, not-for-profit publisher, we work to build communities that sustain and encourage engaging, literary, and current writing.

Called Invisible Publishing until 2026, Invisible Books has been in operation for nearly two decades. We released our first fiction titles in the spring of 2007, and our catalogue has come to include works of graphic fiction and nonfiction, pop culture biographies, experimental poetry, and prose.

We are committed to publishing writers with diverse perspectives. In acknowledging historical and systemic barriers, and the limits of our existing catalogue, we emphatically encourage writers from LGBTQ2SIA+ communities, Indigenous writers, and writers of colour to submit their work.

Invisible Books is also home to the Bibliophonic, Throwback, and DOCUMENTS series.